CLOSING THE DEAL

A SALESPERSON'S DIARY

SHIVA SHANKAR IYER

Made with ♥ on the Notion Press Platform
www.notionpress.com

Family, Friends, Colleagues, Customers.

The Almighty, as always.

Contents

Contents

Acknowledgements

At the time of my working as a Sales Manager, my mother put forth an interesting suggestion to me.

'You keep telling me about this customer and that, what they did and how you handled them. Why don't you maintain a file about these conversations? Maybe in the future, you can look back and laugh at these incidents.'

I started maintaining an Excel sheet, replete with small conversation snippets and diary entries, about how each customer phone call was vastly different from the next.

Today, I am delighted to present those diary entries to you, in the form of a full-fledged book today.

My first thanks would go out to my parents – Shankar and Lakshmi. They provided the guidance and support upon reading multiple drafts and encouraged me to explore more ideas while penning down these stories.

My colleagues in sales and mentors for life, they have taught me a lot. A lot of their experiences and stories have been mixed, blended and presented to you in the form of this book.

Finally, my friends, well-wishers and readers, who had only one question on their minds.

'When is your next book out?'

Vishal, for the amazing creatives and ideas for the book launch.

Moving away from the beaten path – this book would not have been possible without the assistance of my laptop, phone, email and messenger apps. These are the true unsung heroes of this book. I hope authors continue to acknowledge the contribution of technology in their books from this day forward.

-Shiva Shankar Iyer

Why This Book?

I hated everything about sales.

Every time I heard the word sales – the only images which popped up in my mind were credit card selling individuals who only had only three words in their mind – prey, target, attack.

You see these characters in movies and TV shows. Salespersons are depicted as slimy, fast-talking, money-minded animals who want to suck away every single hard-earned rupee of yours.

I was completely shocked at the turn of events when I first started my sales journey – because everything I thought sales was about...was completely true and on the dot. I was genuinely hoping it would be a land of paradise where people were nice to each other and bosses were good-hearted personalities.

So, what is this book about?

As it is, there are multiple books on the market – cold calling, selling techniques, the tele-marketers guide, how to close a difficult customer, so on and so forth. Many advocates of hardcore sales will tell you, that a stint in selling teaches one life skills: how to face rejection, never taking no for an answer, radical thinking to get the month's target done somehow through the BBS method - Beg, Borrow or Steal.

This book is not here to teach you how to sell. Neither is it a book which preaches you a hundred things about the different types of customers out there and how to develop a sales pipeline.

All this book is trying to do - is humanize salespeople through stories. We are human beings, after all. Professionals next, human beings first.

I have found that telling stories is the easiest way to get someone's attention. Building characters, the premise, the middle and the end. Maybe, this is why our ancestors and forefathers sought to impart life lessons through story-telling, instead of writing a 30,000-word textbook on how to live one's life.

Selling has taught me a lot about life. In my short stint as a salesperson, I have always tried to gain the trust of the customer first, before selling the product. This has meant that I have had to go without achieving my target for some months. What stood out for me was valuing my customers more than the incentive at the end of the period.

I may have not hit my target every time, yet I was accomplished within. I personally knew folks who hit their target month on month through hook or by crook...but inside? Completely empty.

I hope you enjoy the ride! Many of you might relate to these anecdotes, either from your personal or professional life.

As always, bouquets and brickbats are equally appreciated.

How To Read This Book?

This book follows the pattern of my previous books: 'GoodForNothingNalayak (2018)' and 'The Nalayak Returns (2021)'. It is in the short story format, which means you can sneak in a story to munch on before bedtime, after bedtime, during chai-time, while travelling in the metro, listening to music, taking bath...ok, maybe not in the bathroom.

Although there is no pre-defined connection with each of the stories, I would recommend reading the book in the chronological order as provided in the index.

I have noticed something interesting about books and reading in general. The same book, read at different points in my life, have meant different things to me. For example, when I read a Harry Potter book back in school, I always thought the books were about magic.

Today, I realize that magic was only the medium. The real strength of the stories lay in its characters and their humanness – good, bad, or ugly.

Similarly, I was not a fan of my sales stint. Day after day, month after month – the routine was deafening. Only when I quit, completed my post-graduation, then sat back to ruminate about the days gone past – did I realize that there was a story to tell and the time had come to put pen to paper. As I have grown as a person (my well-wishers would debate this point), I like to believe that my storytelling has evolved and matured over time.

Consider this book as a light snack, not a five-course meal. You may not even be in sales, yet I'm sure you will be able to relate to one story or the other in this book. You may have been a customer at the other end of the call, even my customer at some point – for crying out loud. You might be a salesperson starting off, or an experienced sales head with glowing battle scars.

Whoever you are, wherever you are – Happy Reading!

A Quick Disclaimer – Before You Begin

This book has been written under the premise that the Covid-19 lockdown is still in place in 2020-21, and none of the offices in India or the World are open. All conversations that take place in the story are either through online meetings, phone calls or messenger apps – in light of the Work from Home directives issued by India Inc., to safeguard the health and well-being of the employees by enforcing social distancing.

None of the conversations or sales pitches occurred in-person.

This is a work of fiction. Unless otherwise indicated, all the names, characters, businesses, places, events and incidents in this book are either the product of the author's imagination or used in a fictitious manner. Any resemblance to actual persons, living or dead, or actual events is purely coincidental.

Sales Cycle At Aspire Learning Solutions

CHAPTER ONE

ENTERING

'Sir, I am from a biotech background. Please reject me,' I pleaded.

'No, Surya. You have done well in all the rounds. Your speaking skills are really good. I want to give you a chance in this job.'

'Thank you, Sir. I really appreciate this. But I have no background in sales or marketing. You would be making a mistake in hiring me.'

I was negotiating with Ajith, the head of Sales and Marketing for Aspire Learning Solutions. It was the last round of the Inside Sales Manager job. I had passed the initial rounds – Group Discussion, summarizing a sales pitch and a written test.

I had given the tests on a whim, since I really had no other skill that any company could use during the Covid-19 pandemic. Maybe, I should have opened that Computer Science book occasionally, instead of using it as a handrest.

I was praying that the final panel would reject me. I was an engineer, what would I do in sales?

'Leave that judgement to me. I want you to accept this offer,' Ajith said.

'Allow me to think about this, Sir. I need a day's time,' I said.

'No problem. Take all the time you need. Just ensure that your onboarding procedures are done by tomorrow, we can start your training immediately,' Ajith said, and logged out of the meeting.

'Was he making the decision for me?' I thought to myself.

I spoke to my mom, dad, and my friends. 'What was the worst that could happen?' was all that they said. 'Leave the job, if you don't like it,' my friend said.

'It's not like you are a contract worker, right?' another said.

'Give it a shot, you might like it,' my parents said.

I made my decision. The reality was, I had no other option.

Who knew, a decision back then would become book material today.

CHAPTER TWO

I WANT TO TALK TO YOUR MANAGER

'Mom, I am not interested. How many times will I repeat the same thing?'

I was in the middle of a customer call, when my Mom interluded with the same sermon once again.

'Surya, an MBA is a good career option. You've already done engineering, why not top it up with a Master's degree?'

'Masters? Mom, I'm working right now, earning good money. People do an MBA to earn money, isn't it? That is already happening. Why would I want to get back to studies again? Besides, who coined the word 'top-up'? I am not recharging my phone now, am I?'

'This boy will never learn. Why waste my energy on him.' Mom said to herself, and left my room.

I was on a call with a very irritating customer. Did I say irritating? I meant *chindi*.

I was working as an assistant sales manager in the Tele-sales division, at an education technology company. We sold online courses and preparatory material to working professionals and students, who were looking to skill up in their respective domains. My job was to educate, convince and cajole them to buy our courses.

It was mostly about how outdated and pre-historic they may become in the next six months, if they do not buy our courses. It wasn't the best-selling tactic, but hey – isn't that how insurance is sold?

'Sir, please understand. 20% off is the only offer I have with me now. My manager will not approve of anything above this.'

'Boss, I am getting the same course from LearnTech at 40% discount. Both of you have the exact same course material and same faculty. Give me 5 reasons why I should come to your platform.'

How about one - I will make my incentive for the month?

'I completely understand your predicament, Sir. But, if you go through the website, you will be paying the full amount. If you agree to pay right away, I will apply a 20% discount on the payment link shared from my end.'

'You will get the same material, at a lower price. Isn't that a good deal?'

The customer was impatient. 'Ok, looks like you will not listen. Maybe next time then.' His voice started to become distant, as I realized he was about to cut the call.

Something struck me.

'Sir, SIR! Just a minute. Please stay on the line.'

'Yes, Surya. What is it? I don't want to waste your time.'

'Absolutely not, Sir. We are not here to waste each other's time. Why don't I ask my manager to call you? It would be great if you could have a one-on-one with my higher-ups.'

This was a sales tactic which had worked incredibly for me. Customers refuse to talk to the salesperson regarding discounts, offers and payment terms. They want to be given importance throughout the sales cycle, which is practically impossible for a sales manager to do, since she/he will be managing multiple accounts at a time, each more devilish than the next.

So, how does one resolve such a predicament?

Simple. I used the Manager *astra*.

'Hmm...I will talk to your manager, fine. What good will that come out of this?'

'Sir, why don't I arrange a call immediately? I don't have the authority to release more discount, probably you could convince my manager and argue your case.'

The customer fell for it. Classic sweep.

'Yeah sure, ask your manager to call me in the next ten minutes. I have a meeting on my calendar.'

'Sure Sir, let me do that.'

I disconnected the call, and waited for twenty minutes.

The customer noticed his phone ringing. It was from an unknown number. He picked up the call.

'Ranadeep De? This is Kapil Dewan from Aspire Solutions.'

'Hi Kapil, how are you? I believe I asked Surya to call me within 10 minutes.' Ranadeep started.

'I believe you had asked for some leeway regarding the discount on the Microsoft Cloud course, is my understanding correct?' Kapil spoke, in a very gruff voice.

Ranadeep seemed taken aback. 'Umm...yes. I did speak to Surya regarding this...'

'Mr. De, I am sure you are well aware, that we are the leaders in facilitating online trainings, and we have the best faculty as well. From your history on our website, it seems you have seen our complimentary videos on Azure quite a number of times. Well, am I correct in saying you like our content?'

'Kapil look, I was just browsing...'

'Browsing for 4 hours 23 minutes? I can see that you have done activity on our Cloud Masters courses as well.

Are you by chance looking to become a Cloud Architect?'

Ranadeep felt he was losing a grip on the conversation. 'Yes, well that is the plan as of now. Let's see in the future how things go. Right now, what I want is a discount...'

Kapil was refusing to allow Ranadeep to complete. 'Mr. De, I will make you an offer you cannot refuse. Instead of purchasing the standalone Cloud Azure course worth Rs.15,999 – I will allow Surya to sell the Cloud Masters Course to you for Rs.40,999, all-inclusive of GST. You will get 6 courses in total, all rolled up at a discounted price exclusively for you.'

I could feel Ranadeep's eyes widen. 'Really? But what about the website price?'

'Buddy, listen to me. Do you want the course or not? I am not authorized to sell the course at this price, but you seem to be a nice guy. I like you.'

'Yes, of course! I will take the course right away. I wonder why Surya did not mention this to me before.'

'Thank you so much Kapil. How do I proceed now?'

'Surya will help you out. I have another call coming, catch you later Mr. De,' Kapil disconnected the call.

Ranadeep immediately dialled my number.

'Hey Surya, how are you?' Ranadeep started

'I'm fine, Sir. Thank you for asking. I guess you rang me up to inform that you will not be taking the course, right?'

'What nonsense! I just spoke to your manager...wonderful chap. Let's close the deal for the Azure Masters course for Rs.40,999. Send me the link right away, I will pay in full.'

'Wow...sir – may I know what happened on that call? That is a completely different course.'

'Forget all that, Surya. I want the Master's course. And I want it now. Send me the payment link.'

'Sure Sir, I will share the link to your email id. Let me know once you receive it, I will apprise you on further steps.'

Once the deal was closed, I lay down on my sofa.

'Kapil, thanks buddy. I owe you one.' I patted my back.

You guessed it right.

I was Kapil, with just a different number and a different voice!

CHAPTER THREE

WHERE IS YOUR PIPELINE?

'Vijay, I am going to get screwed. Cover for me, *na.*'

'Are you nuts? Why should I get my ass burnt when you guys are not getting me sales? Shut up and join the call.' Vijay, my team lead, smirked.

I was having a bad day, and a bad week.

I was hoping that the Earth would open up and swallow me. We were about to have our daily sales meeting in 10 minutes, and I was in no mood to join the call. Abhishek, our company's Business Manager; and Anuj, the company's co-founder was due to be present in the meeting. Anuj was part of the Founder's Office in charge of operational duties, but he insisted he loved the sales part of the job so much that he used to join our daily sales meetings to discuss leads, targets, and everything in between.

'Look at these morning shift people. They are hunting on our leads like wolves. If they take all our pots, what the heck are we going to tell Abhishek?' Prem whined.

Pots was the shortened form of 'Potential' - in sales parlance. A potential was a lead generated by the system from customer activity on the Aspire website, or else created by a sales agent in the event a customer contacted the agent directly. Good pots could make you the Kingmaker; bad pots could lead you to scraping the bottom of the pan at the end of the month.

Prem was the *jugaadu* of our team. He was known as the Ladies Man, since it was part of Aspire Learning's folklore that he could talk his way to making any lady customer purchase a course on the company website. There was nothing called a tough customer for Prem, only a one who paid.

Let me give you a small introduction to my sales team.

Our team was named – OG4, or Operating Group 4. We were one of the teams operating in the afternoon shift, working from 2 PM-11 PM. In the noon and late evening, we would sell to India. Post 10 PM, the US and the UK markets would be the customers we would prey on.

OG4 typically oversaw selling all Python Programming and Project Management courses. Sounds glamourous? Trust me, nothing could be further than the truth.

'Prem, Abhishek doesn't care where and how you get the sale, as long as you get it. Beg, Borrow and Sell is his idea of meeting targets.' Vijay said.

'Yeah, yeah. I know. Anyway, time's up. Surya, get ready for *bamboo*.'

Bamboo was when the senior management affectionately squeezed, ripped apart and minced a salesperson's confidence within a span of 60 seconds.

I had not done my target on any given day, since the past 15 days. Bye, bye incentive.

I clicked on the Google Meet link. I could see Abhishek and Anuj were already in the call.

What did they have to be punctual every time I had not done my target?

'Hi team. Good noon to everyone. How's it going?' Anuj asked cheerfully.

'No *bamboo*? That's weird.' I thought to myself.

'Everybody switch on your camera. Show me your lovely faces.' Anuj said.

Reluctantly, everyone switched on their laptop cameras. Droopy and sleepy faces adorned the meeting's foreground.

'Hi Anuj, we are good. How are you?' Vijay asked.

'Raman, do you have any payments for today?' Abhishek asked, cutting Vijay short.

Raman was the senior most salesperson on the team. He had developed an enviable reputation of dealing with tough customers and achieving targets under extreme pressure during month-ends. I held him in great respect since he had personally mentored me when I joined the company, hand-holding me from my tenure as an intern to a full-time employee.

Raman was a gentleman par excellence, who had never scammed a customer on a deal. Abhishek seemed to think otherwise.

'Hi Abhishek. I have a few potentials lined up, hopefully, they should pay in the evening.' Raman said.

'Why evening, Raman? What is wrong with the afternoon?'

'Many of the pots said they log in for the afternoon shift at their workplace. Once they are free in the evening, they said they will initiate the payment from their end.'

'Raman, listen. I don't want any excuses. I want these pots paid by 4 PM. You will personally drop a mail to me on the status of these payments.'

'Sure, Abhishek. I will do that.'

I squirmed in my seat.

'Prem, what about you? Where are your payments?' Anuj asked.

'Anuj, hi. How are you?'

I could hear Vijay stifle his laughter through his mike.

'I'm good, Prem. Thank you for asking. *Ab batao*, payments?'

'I have a Masters payment coming up in about 1 hour. Additionally, there is a group deal for the upcoming batch of PMP. Hopefully, they should pay by end of day today.'

'*Wah*, Prem! Great, good job. See guys, learn from him. This is what I call a good salesperson. Prem, well done. Make sure those payments come today itself. Close them with more discount if you have to, but close them. Maintain ticket size as well.'

'Yes, Anuj. I will.'

I could not control my laughter. Prem had confidently bluffed his way through this meeting, and the whole team knew it. The Masters payment he said was forthcoming had blasted him 2 days back for promising a batch which wasn't listed on the company website.

The group deal for PMP was Raman's payment, which was not due to be paid for another 2 weeks, since the pots were awaiting company approval.

'Who laughed? Who is laughing, I say?' Abhishek screamed.

Shit, I'm screwed.

'Surya, what do you have for today?' Anuj asked.

'Umm, Anuj, actually the thing is...'

'What, Surya? Answer Anuj's question.' Abhishek thundered. I could see the sweat on his shiny pate.

'I'm building a pipeline, Anuj.'

'You're building a pipeline?'

'Yes, I'm building a pipeline.' I repeated. It sounded stupid, but I tried to make it look believable.

'Do we look like idiots?'

Did he want an honest answer?

'No, Anuj. I'm not sure why you are getting that impression.'

Anuj lost his cool. 'You have not done your daily target for 15 days in a row. And now, you come and tell me that you are building a pipeline? Do you want your incentive this month or not?'

'Yes, Anuj. I'm trying my best. I had 4 payments lined up this week, but all of them cancelled and went to our competition, Resilient Knowledge, since they offer better discounts and support...'

'Again, with the bloody excuses. What are we paying you for? To eat peanuts?'

'We sell courses! Online courses, for crying out loud. What is this pipeline business? You work for an infrastructure company?'

'Vijay! Where are you?'

'Yes, Anuj. I'm here.' Vijay replied, calmly.

'I want Surya to be working 12 hours a day from now on. Make him login early, log out late; I don't care. If he is not doing his target, then it means that you are not doing your target. Create a report for this guy and make him hunt on old leads.'

'Shut his fresh leads for now, we will take a call based on how the situation goes.'

'Sure Anuj. I will do the needful.'

I closed my eyes. Sales was a demanding job. There was no concept such as log in time, or log out time. If you have done your target, you are the hero of that day.

The very next day that you go on zero, the wolves will hunt for your blood.

'Team, please stay back after Abhishek and Anuj leave.' Vijay said.

The meeting was silent. Vijay cleared his throat and spoke.

'So, Surya. Ready for *bamboo* from tomorrow?'

'Vijay, what do I say? I'm doing everything I can. My pots are not responding to my calls, emails, or texts. Everyone wants a discount and Resilient is giving it. Companies are not ready to reimburse due to cost cutting and trimming down on employee upskilling costs.'

'Really, this is a shit job.'

'Chill, dude. It's all part of the job. Prem and Raman have been through hundreds of calls like this, they're still here.'

'Guys, help Surya to achieve at least 80% of his target this month. Be his manager, Subject Matter Expert or whatever. Just get the job done.'

'Yes boss.' Prem quipped.

'I'll handle Abhishek and Anuj in the next meeting. But Surya, I need you to commit that you will put extra efforts to do your target.'

'Sure, Vijay. I will do it.'

I didn't do my target that month.

The very next month, I achieved 200% of my target. Abhishek personally called to congratulate me.

I logged into our daily sales meeting to discuss the past month performance.

'Congrats guys. The team has done its target, proud of you all. Surya, good job and keep the payments flowing.'

Anuj suddenly pivoted to Prem.

'So, Prem. No payments, huh? What's your story?'

Prem smiled.

'I'm building a pipeline. Anuj.'

The bluff continues. Till next time!

CHAPTER FOUR

MY KIDS ARE IN NURSERY

It was month end. That time of the month.

The entire sales met at 8 AM in the morning and worked 16 hours round the clock till 12 AM the next day, to meet the company's month end target.

This month was particularly tense for me, as I needed only about Rs.12,500 to achieve my target and grab my incentive.

Incentives were good. Sometimes, I earned double my basic salary when I did well.

I was dealing with a particularly tough customer, who was refusing to buy our Big Data Hadoop course.

'Sir, try to understand. I have already given you the maximum discount possible. My manager will not agree to any other price.'

'Boss, listen. I am getting a better deal at Evergreen Learning. And those guys are giving me a free course as well with the entire bundle. I am only talking to you because a friend recommended that the course material from Aspire Solutions is top notch.'

My ears perked up. This was a classic case of a customer, who wanted to take the course, but was hesitant to proceed because the price was out of his budget. Generally, customers are seen to show aggression to cover their helplessness.

'Sir, I have to tell you something.' I said, timing my words slowly.

'Yeah? What's that?' the customer said.

'You know that this is the end of the month, right?'

'Thank you for reminding me. I keep a calendar at home, but maybe I should call you for the date and time whenever I'm in doubt!' he guffawed.

Idiot.

'I have 2 wives and 2 kids, sir. My situation is not good.'

'Oh... I could sense that his snarky attitude had dropped.

'Yes Sir. I have to send my kids to nursery school. Tomorrow, their fees is due. I have two kids, one boy and one girl. We are planning for two more, Sir.'

'With your blessings and kindness, I will be able to pay the school fees tomorrow with my sales incentive this month.'

'Please buy this course, Sir, then I will be able to achieve my target and receive my incentive.'

I had kept my Engineering Marks card next to me, just in case. Looking at it always made me cry. This time round as well, it worked.

'Please Sir, I want to educate my children. The donation for nursery school is so high, what do I even say. Two lakhs per child, *aiyoo*,' I started to wail loudly.

'Hey, hey, buddy – listen. I'm sorry to hear about your situation. Let me pay now, ok? Forget the discount. Leave it. I will pay directly from the website, and I will make sure that you get your incentives.'

'Sir, you don't have to do that Sir...'

'I'm paying now, alright? I'm already on the website payment page and have selected my batch. My 3 other friends wanted to join the course with me, so I'm going to pay for them as well.'

Shit. This guy was a group deal account? My lucky day.

'Done, I've made the payment. Is it reflecting in your system?'

I checked my CRM for the status of the payment.

'Yes Sir, it's done. Thank you so much for your kindness and consideration. How can I ever repay you?'

'Hey, no worries, man. Just make sure that your kids go to school. Education is important for a person's future.'

'Sir, I will name my third child after you. You are great.'

'Yeah, now things are getting weird. All the best man, you've achieved your target for this month. Enjoy the rest of the day. Bye, Bye.'

I did feel a little bad for the customer, he was nice.

I was awarded the 'Dazzling Performer' award for closing four payments on a month-end day, along with achieving my target. I silently said a 'Thank you' to that wonderful gentleman, who decided that humanity was much bigger than saving a few rupees in discounts.

CHAPTER FIVE

GOKU BUYS A COURSE

I was sitting in front of my laptop, browsing through my leads to find potential payments. I could find none. My calls for the day weren't looking promising as well. I had to follow-up on leads who had not bothered to return my calls or messages, the standard excuses being:

'Oh, sorry Surya. I have postponed my learning plans due to a restructuring in my organisation.'

Translation: The customer was getting kicked out of the company, and buying a new course was the last thing on his mind.

'My manager has not approved the budget for the course. Let's connect in six months' time...I want the course at the same discount!'

Translation: I am not really interested in buying your course, but it looks useful for my appraisal. My manager is funding his Thailand trip with our course money, so too bad I won't be able to go ahead with the purchase.

To make matters worse, it was the month of March in Bangalore, where summers can get pretty brutal. I had just taken a bath, but it seemed like I needed another one as I wiped the sweat off my forehead.

My Gmail inbox pinged. A new lead had been assigned to me.

Typically, new leads assigned to sales agents have the following information – email id, phone number, activity done on our company website and their potential course of interest. We also had a tool to check their background, so that we could pitch the course to them according to their skill levels and educational qualifications.

The main funda for using the background check tool, was to check whether the pot had the capacity to pay for the course or not.

'Okay, let me check out the new lead. Hopefully, my day should turn around quickly.' I prayed.

'So, email id is...what? You can't be serious.'

'*saiyangoku999@gmail.com*? What kind of email id is this?'

I quickly used my background check tool and punched in the email id provided by the pot.

'Saurav Pandey, 9th standard student, Modern High School, Kolkata,' the details ran.

I wrung my hands. How the hell was I supposed to make a sale if these were the types of leads I received? I was part of a team which sold Python and related courses. As it is, our conversion rate was languishing at a measly 5%, for which our team used to get battered by the management on our daily sales calls.

Now, with high school students doing activity on our courses, we were done for. Students have a great level of curiosity, but zero ability to pay. Parents would never allow their kids to enrol for a Python course worth Rs.15,000, justifying that there is so much free content on the internet, why waste money here.

To top it all, social media and other forms of news were abound with how upskilling in programming languages such as Python and C++ were the quickest way to achieve *nirvana*. Forget Python, these kids needed to grow a moustache first before taking over the world.

Heck, which 9th grade kid would even have a bank account to start with?

I thought to myself. If I didn't initiate the call to the kid, my manager would be sure to audit my calls and send out a flurry of questions in my direction – mostly about compliance, quality checks and company policy. Audit checks generally go with random sampling, and somehow my call records were always the ones which tended to be picked out. I wondered what kind of game probability was playing with me.

I had made my decision. I picked up my phone, logged in the kid's number into the system, and made the call.

'Hi, is this Saurav?'

'Yes Sir,' a squeaky voice spoke from the other end of the line.

'Hi Saurav, this is Surya from Aspire Solutions. I noticed that you have shown interest in the Python Programming course on our website. I am sure that you must have some questions regarding the curriculum, course material and the instructors.'

'Anything I can assist you with?' I spoke in a monotone, having spoken this rehearsed line to over a hundred customers and counting.

'No, I don't have any questions. I am looking at your website now, I want to join the Aug 31st batch, which is a weekend.'

I took a pause. 'Okay, so the kid seems interested.' I thought to myself.

'Ok, sure Saurav. I have just checked the dates and details in my system, we seem to have a few slots open for the mentioned dates. Would you like me to check you in for the Aug 31st batch?'

'Yes Sir. I want to join.'

Hmm, interesting. Now comes the part where the kid would haggle for discounts.

'Sure, I can check you in. What would be your mode of payment?'

'You need to have a bank account to pay buddy. Go home and play Road Rash or something,' I thought to myself.

'Yeah, I have 3 credit cards – American Express: AMEX, Bank of America, and HSBC. Which one would you like me to use?'

I was drinking a glass of water while the kid was talking. I spat out the water on the wall just above my laptop screen.

'I'm sorry, what? You have three credit cards? All international banks?' I said, bewildered.

'Yes Sir. Can you send me the payment link?'

'Umm, Saurav – can you confirm if you will be paying for the course? Can you check if your Mom or Dad are around, they can do the transaction.'

'Sir, these are my cards. I will be doing the payment. The total price of the course is Rs.17,559 without GST, and with the GST it is Rs.20,719. I have done the math before giving my details.'

'Do you mind sending me the link now? I have to leave for my math tuitions in 10 minutes.'

My head went into a spin, but I composed myself. Here's a kid, with 3 credit cards, knows the course cost, and has not bothered to negotiate for any discounts. How lucky could I get?

'Okay Saurav, fair enough. The interest rates on the AMEX card seem favourable, so let me initiate a payment link from my end with the corresponding details. You can pay now, you're sure?'

'Yes. Sir. Send. Now.' It seemed like he was nearing the end of his patience level.

'This is your email id? _saiyangoku999@gmail.com_?' I confirmed once again.

'Yes, that's the one.'

I sent the link across, with a validity of 15 minutes. It was my lucky day, I felt flowers fall all over me.

'Thanks, I have received the link. I will pay now.' Saurav said, and hung up.

An entire hour passed by.

Complete radio silence from Saurav. I had my apprehensions before sending the payment link to a 9th grade kid, but he seemed to have me convinced.

I called Saurav up. This time, a gruff voice picked up the phone.

'Hi Saurav, did you...' I started.

Before I could complete my sentence, a man on the other line started to scream at the top of his voice.

'What kind of company are you running? Sending payment links to small kids? Are you not ashamed of yourself? This boy has taken all my credit cards and has been going around shopping on different websites. You should have some common sense before talking to such kids.'

'If this every happens again, I will make sure to call the police and close down your company. Utter nonsense behaviour, *thoo*,' he spat into the phone and hung up the call.

I stared at my computer screen, with no thoughts crossing my head. An unpaid payment link, fooled by a kid. Having an unpaid link in Abhishek's team was akin to going into a lion's cave and convincing it to become vegetarian. I was going to be the joke in my group for the next one week.

My Gmail inbox pinged.

'*doraemon488@yahoo.com* has shown interest in the Python for Data Science course.'

Audit checks were not so bad after all. It's all about perspective.

CHAPTER SIX

It's our Anniversary, Sir.

A salesperson doesn't just sell courses.

We sell dreams, hopes, ambition and promise. But mostly, we sell greed to the customers.

'The packages expected post completing this course are in the ballpark of Rs.25-30 lakhs per annum.' I said.

'Really? Wow, that sounds amazing,' a customer said happily.

'Absolutely. But you have to understand that this depends on the market conditions, growth potential for the skillset you possess, compounded annual growth rate of the industry and of course, the prevailing economic and political conditions.' I threw in multiple jargons as a disclaimer, but making it sound less ominous by using lengthier words.

'You will be in the top 10% of the industry by 2028 if you buy this course. It really is your call – if you want to become CEO or not.' I concluded.

This pitch was being sold to an 8th class kid. I'm not sure if he was even eligible to drive or vote.

It was a regular day, when I was going through my prospect list and looking out for any upcoming payments. My list did not look promising.

I knew that Abhishek would be after my life if I did not get at least two payments today. I was already Number 1 on his hitlist and he was itching for a chance to move me out of his team. He was not a very fun guy to work with, lest hang out with.

Abhishek was the type of person who would ask why Dettol could not guarantee 100% of germ protection. 'They are being too complacent with just 99.99%. It shows that they are not ambitious at all. The company does not have the makings of a great organization,' he would say.

I realized that there were no payments coming my way, hence I had to opt for an alternate strategy, one which I absolutely hated and detested.

Cold calling pots and selling them dreams.

A lot of people assume that cold calling is not effective - they are not completely wrong. Cold calling is generally given to new joiners before they can be onboarded to their sales teams; it is more like a rite of passage. Closing a sale from Overdue pots or Closed Lost pots (disqualified as a prospect by the sales agent after multiple follow-ups) meant that you displayed the tenacity of a good salesperson, making over 200 calls a day, just to zero in on one potential person who 'might' pay.

And, that's a very, very doubtful *might*.

I quickly created a report in my CRM dashboard of all the pots who were Closed Lost and Overdue. I applied multiple filters for the courses where the propensity to pay was higher – Power BI, Cloud Computing courses, Full Stack Developer....and so on. I applied a filter for recent pots who were disqualified or left for dead by the sales agents. 'Three months should be a good timeline,' I thought to myself.

Satisfied, I ran the report.

The system blurted out a stunning number.

550 pots.

This was an impossible task to do in one day. I attempted to filter the pots by experience; higher the experience of the pot in the industry, the probability of them wanting to skill up would be higher. At least, that was the assumption I was running with.

'Hello Sir? Hi, how are you? This is Surya from Aspire, hope you are having a good day.'

The customer's name was Prashant Padke, a software engineer with a major IT firm in Pune. He had about 6 years of experience in testing and a few years as a project manager. I was attempting to sell him a Masters Course in Software Testing.

'You called me now. Of course, it's not a good day anymore,' he grunted.

'Ha ha, good one Sir.' I cursed him under my breath.

'May I have two minutes of your time, Sir?'

'What do you want? I am busy in a meeting.' Prashanth said.

This was the point when I understood the play. If he was busy in a meeting, he would never have picked my call. Even if he had picked up my call by mistake, he has not cut it yet. This was my cue to start my pitch.

'Sir, as you know Software testing is poised for a significant evolution, driven by emerging technology and industry trends. Artificial Intelligence and Machine Learning are being integrated into the development environments rapidly that the lead time for the Software Development Life Cycle has reduced exponentially. Validating AI based algorithms and interoperability with Internet of Things eco-systems, makes software testing an exciting field to be in at the moment.'

'Come to the point. I know all of this. *Baap ko mat sikha*,' Prashanth said.

'Sure Sir. I noticed that you had shown interest in the Masters Course for Software Testing. We have an upcoming batch on April 15th, would you like to enrol in the same? We have few seats left, but I would be happy to accommodate you in the upcoming one.'

'Keep the seats to yourself. Thank you, and goodbye.' I heard his voice fade away.

My brain hit the pause button.

The guy heard me out, full pitch and all. He had shown interest in the course a few months back, and was marked as Closed Lost. For this guy's profile, marking him as a lost cause did not make sense. I had a gut feeling he knew all about the course, but something was holding him back.

Did he not like the syllabus? Did he not like the infrastructure and material we provided?

Then, it hit me like a thunderbolt.

There was only one obvious answer.

'Sir, Sir, WAIT! I had called you regarding an offer on the course, as we celebrate Aspire's 5th anniversary.'

I heard a few seconds of silence on the other line. I could feel my heart pumping.

'Anniversary?'

'Yes, Sir. Aspire has completed 5 years in the Education Tech marketplace, and we are holding a weeklong celebration in office.'

'In office? Aren't all of you guys working from home due to Covid? Which office is open now?'

'No Sir, I meant office in the general sense of the word. Office is a feeling, it's an emotion. In fact, employees make up an office. Without the employees, there is no office.'

Prashanth chuckled. 'Yeah, yeah. Alright. Tell me about this offer.'

My hunch was right. I proceeded.

'We are providing you a 40% discount on all Masters course of your choice, and a self-paced course free. It goes without saying that all the courses will be of a lifetime access and 24x7 tech and subject matter support will be provided to you.'

'Hmm, that's not a bad offer. You know, the guy before you did not have the courtesy to even offer me a 15% discount the last time I spoke to your company. He kept on selling me some bullshit about value over cost. I mean, boss – this is India. I will extract the maximum value possible out of the course at minimum cost. Doesn't mean that I some sort of a *chindi,* just saying.'

'The last guy wasn't desperate, I am,' I thought to myself.

'Anyways, tell me something. What date is Aspire's Anniversary?'

'Umm...3rd April, Sir.' I said, with some hesitation in my voice.

'Oh, is it? When I drop a Google Search for your company's history, why does it say that the company was founded on 29th November 2016'?

Shit, this guy was smart. I changed gears immediately.

'Yes Sir, that is correct. We officially opened our first office on April 3rd 2017, so the company celebrates a dual anniversary on both the dates.'

'What? That makes absolutely no sense.'

I'm just a career counsellor, Sir – what can I say about when the company conducts its celebrations. We just do our job,' I said apologetically.

Prashanth didn't seem to buy my cock-and-bull story, but decided against pursuing that line of questioning.

'Ok, let's leave that discussion. Come back to Masters Course. What is your final price?'

'So, as you can see – the website price is Rs.69,999 without GST, with 18% GST the course price comes to Rs.82,599. Since we are applying a 40% discount, the final payable course fee would be Rs.49,560. You would be getting a self-paced course free as well, of your choice.'

'Okay, this sounds good. I can pay you in 2-3 days' time. Keep the offer on hold for me until then. *Chalo*, nice talking to you, bye bye.'

'Prashanth, wait!'

'I'm sorry, what?'

I did not want the *bamboo* from Abhishek. I had to close this guy.

'I meant, Prashanth *Sir*, wait. The Anniversary offer ends today.'

'How can it end today? You said it yourself, the anniversary was on April 3rd, today is April 6th. If it is a weeklong celebration, I have time till at least April 10th, isn't that, right?'

This customer was very *chalu*. My weapons arsenal was running out as I was caught in my own web of lies.

'Well, we have another offer over the Anniversary offer. Would you like to hear that?'

'Oh yeah? What's this one all about?'

'So, if you enrol at any time halfway through the Anniversary, you will be getting two self-paced courses free. I have special permission from my region head to execute this offer just for you.'

'Dude, seriously. What kind of offer is this?'

'It's the company, Sir. I'm just an employee doing my job.'

'Tell your marketing department to come up with better offers. Do me a favour, make the course price as Rs.45,000 flat, inclusive of GST – I will pay right away.'

'Umm, well....'

'No? Okay, fine. Next time maybe. See you later.'

I was going to bang my head against a wall. My ticket size would be screwed, I would be blasted for giving this level of discounts, but what the heck – I was going to close Prashanth.

'*Arre yaar*, wait Sir, wait please. Why are you always in a hurry?'

'Can I talk to my manager, please? He has to approve this offer.'

'Ok, go ahead. Call me on this number on your final decision.'

I took of my headset, and closed my laptop. By the end of fifteen minutes, I had relieved myself, washed my face and had a glass of orange juice. The manager had made his decision.

'Hey Prashanth, hi. I have spoken to my manager. As a special case, he is willing to extend you the Masters Course on Software Testing at the agreed price of Rs.45,000.'

'That's great. How do I pay?'

'Prashanth, before proceeding – I would like to ask you for a favour.'

'What's that?'

'This is a very tight offer for me. I will most probably lose out my incentive on this deal. Of course, I would like to give this to you since I have already committed an offer.'

'I would like you to make a Gentleman's Agreement with me.'

Prashanth was taken aback. 'One second, what is this all about?'

'I would like you to refer two of your friends to enrol at Aspire Solutions. And when they decide to take up a course, they don't go to the website – they come straight to me. You can share my contact details with them.'

'I will ensure you earn some Aspire Reward coins as a referral bonus. Do we have a deal?'

Prashanth thought for a while. He seemed to be thinking over this quite seriously.

He replied:

'I am good to go with this. Send me the payment link and EMI options for credit card. Let's do this.'

Two months later, Prashanth texted me that two of his colleagues would like to take up training on Project Management courses from our website. That very month, I ended up doing 150% of my target.

Was Prashanth the only reason I ended up hitting my target slab? No, not really.

Sometimes, trust between a customer and a salesperson is a bind which transcends any kind of legal document or email. It is sacrosanct.

Until... he gets a better discount from somewhere else!

CHAPTER SEVEN

'Dude, I don't want your course, Godammit!

My afternoon work timings coincide with the meal times of Indian professionals and while evening approaches, the crucial Western market of the United States wakes up.

We face a lot of competition from the morning shift of different business units – who target the Eastern markets and our leads as well. I can tell you for a fact that many egos have been bruised as agents try to poach potential sales from other salesperson's territory. The afternoon shift leads were the most sought after, since our work timings overlapped with a few hours of US work timings.

Clearly, selling a course to a person based in the US meant that the ticket size of the course would be captured in US dollars, which was worth almost 3 sales to an Indian client.

'Raman bhai, I got a US lead. Should I call?'

Raman was the go-to person for me on any calls. It was the first time that I was calling a US pot. It had been five months on the floor for me till date, and I was confident of handling Indian clients.

Foreign clients? Not so much.

'Sure, call this guy. Where is this person based out of?'

'Umm...let me check. His name is Robert Kelling, based out of New York. Email id is rob.genesis344@gmail.com, and he has provided a phone number as well. As of last night, he has watched our tutorial video on the website and downloaded the curriculum as well.'

'Did you say last night?' Raman asked.

'Yes, last night.' I let that linger for a bit. Why is the timing important?

'Listen, Surya. Call the pot now. It's already 10.30 PM IST, so this person is probably active in the US. Call him immediately and update the lead, before the Night shift gets a wind of this.'

'On it, Raman bhai.'

'What's this guy's profile?'

I opened up my Sales Navigator and checked Rob's profilc.

'Well, he has four years of experience in testing services and automation.'

'Seems like a good profile. Call this guy fast and ask him what he wants.'

I updated the lead, and initiated a call to Rob. A robot-like female voice spoke that Rob was not available at the moment, and asked me to leave a message.

'Hey Rob, hope you are doing well. I'm Surya from the Aspire team. I had tried reaching you on your personal number to discuss your course interests, but it looks like you are not available at the moment.'

'Could you call me back at your earliest convenient time? Thanks.' I ended the call.

As per statutory procedure, I dropped an email with the course links and syllabus of the content he was interested in, along with my WhatsApp number – in the event he wanted to connect further.

I put my follow-up date as tomorrow, and forgot about the lead.

The next day, I initiated another call from my end. Again, the robotic female voice answered.

I put a follow-up date for three days from now. 'Maybe he is tied up in some office work,' I thought to myself.

Three days later, I gave another attempt. The robot lady answered again.

I went wild. Who was this person and why was he playing games with me? I had done multiple follow-ups and dropped multiple emails.

Did he not know how to use a computer or answer a phone?

'Let me try one last time. If he doesn't answer the call, I will close this guy's lead forever. The other shifts can hunt on him.'

I called his number 3-4 times in a row. I played a hunch that he was not going to pick up my call anyway, so I tried my luck. At least I would have reached my daily call target for the day.

I rang his number the fifth time, and this time – someone picked up.

'Hello? Hi Rob, this is Surya from…'

'What the heck is your problem man? I don't want your course, Godammit! Stop calling me again and again, or I will sue your company and take you to court on grounds of harassment.'

'Yes, but - you showed interest in our testing courses, and…'

'You know what? Take this interest and shove it where it belongs.'

'Don't you ever call me ever again.' He slammed the phone down.

Harassment? What was this guy talking about?

In India, this was called persistence.

I spoke to my lead, Vijay about the call. He roared with laughter; I could almost see the tears rolling down his face.

'You know, I heard the recording of the call. It was hilarious. But hearing it from you was way funnier.'

'Why did Rob have to behave like that? I was just doing my job.' I said.

'Yes, there is something you need to know about US customers. If they want a course, they will come after you to purchase it. If they don't want it – trust me, they will never give you their business how much ever hard you try.'

'What about Indian professionals?' I asked.

'Yeah, these guys are a different ball game. You have to pursue, bargain, and cajole the Indian customer into buying your product – until they make up their mind.'

'Different countries, different customers.' Vijay concluded.

'So...then what do I do? Should I just 'Close-Lost' the lead?'

'No. You drop a mail, and then you make one phone call. The pot doesn't pick up, fine. Drop a WhatsApp. Then you wait.'

'You wait, until they show interest again on the website. Now, you have every right to reach out to them and counsel them on their course of interest. This time, the pot will listen to you and even help you close the deal even if it means they have to shell out a little more money than necessary.'

'Wow, Vijay. You are amazing. How did you learn so much in so little time?'

'I have an American girlfriend. Don't you know?'

'No, not really. She told you all this?'

'I figured it out. Most of my sales used to be from her friend's circle.'

'Oh? And I thought business and pleasure could never go together. Hi-fi to that!'

Vijay didn't seem to find it funny.

CHAPTER EIGHT

LADKI MILEGI?

I worked in the 2-11 PM shift. It was close to 10.45 PM, and I was mentally preparing myself to hit the sack in 15 minutes.

'What a shitty day. Not a single sale. Hopefully tomorrow gets better.' I mumbled to myself.

Suddenly, Aspire's call centre number flashed onto my mobile. This was an incoming enquiry call; someone had looked up the number on our website and had some doubts to clarify. Although the call was dialled to the company number, it was routed to the nearest available sales agent at that point of time.

'If I don't pick up the call, Abhishek will take my case the next day. Heck, let's talk to this person and get it done with.'

The call centre number was connected to our CRM system, so all calls were recorded and the time stamp would be displayed as well. I took the call.

'Thank you for reaching Aspire Solutions, how can I assist you today?'

'Hello...?' the voice sounded distant.

'Hi, this is Surya from Aspire Solutions. How can I assist you today?'

'Hello, *Bhaiyya*?'

'Yes Sir?'

'How much?' he asked.

Until this point, my mind was on autopilot and switch off mode. I rubbed my eyes hard and slapped myself awake. 'This customer might pay right now, Surya it's your lucky night!' I grinned.

'Sure Sir, I can assist you on this. May I know which course you would like to purchase?'

'Shakila madam. How much?' he repeated.

'What the...?'

'How much, *Bhaiyya*?'

The guy sounded pitch drunk, and by the looks of it – he has assumed our company to be a centre for call girls. I decided to have some fun.

'Sir, for one night: 25,000 only.' I said.

'One night? 25,000, *Bhaiyya*?'

'Yes Sir. You want?'

'*Bhaiyya*, give good rate *Bhaiyya*.'

'Okay, okay. You want to talk to my manager? I give you the number.'

'Yes, yes. Tell me, *Bhaiyya*.'

'Note down the number,' I said.

'One...'

'Yes...one...after that?'

'Zero...'

'Zero...ok, then?'

'Zero...' I said gruffly.

'One...Zero...Zero. Hey, this is the police number,' he said.

'Yes Sir. The Assistant Commissioner of Bangalore is my superior. You can call him for a good rate for Shakila madam.'

Before I could say another word, the customer hung up the phone.

What a way to end the night! I saved the recording and our team had a good laugh over the nocturnal phone call.

CHAPTER NINE

MONTH END-MOTIVATION AND MAYHEM-PART 1

Shit, I hated month-ends.

Month-ends are a time which every salesperson hated, depending on where they were with respect to their sales targets.

Targets were divided into Slabs, with the target increasing with every subsequent slab.

If an agent had completed their Slab 1, they were good – not good enough.

If an agent had completed their Slab 2, they were good enough, but not the best.

If an agent had done their Slab 3...well, help the team! Do you think sales is only about you?

In sales, there is no such thing as enough sales, or target achieved. There was always another sale to be made, another potential customer to be converted and another referral to be encashed.

'Soumik bhai, how much do you have to complete your Slab 2?' I asked.

Soumik whistled quietly, as he thought aloud. 'So, my Slab 1 was 6 lakhs, now for Slab 2; I have to make around 2-3 sales, then I'll be done with it. How about you?'

'Bro, my scene is not great. I still have 62k more to achieve my Slab 1. I don't make it here; Abhishek will dump me in the PIP. He badly wants to see me there.'

PIP, or Performance Improvement Program was also known as the 'Toothpaste.'

Why, Toothpaste?

Have you ever tried squeezing out paste from the tube, and putting the exact same quantity back in?

Impossible, right?

PIP was something similar. You were given an impossible target to achieve in a span of 10 days. Within these 10 days, if you were unable to achieve the given target – you would be on your way out.

'Nah, don't worry about it. The team is short-staffed anyway. You'll be in the team, no doubt. Just give your best shot today.'

It was the 30th of April. I had slogged and slogged the entire month, to achieve just over 3 lakhs in revenue. My incentives were tied to the slabs or targets laid out by the company, so not achieving the month's slab meant my phone's EMI downpayment would get postponed again.

This was a tough month to begin with. The market was rough, customers were postponing their learning journeys and companies were downsizing. But the management didn't care anyway. Whenever a salesperson complained that the market was dry and competitors were cutting our leads, this is what the leadership had to say-

'Are you making enough calls? Let's go through your call registry together.'

'You aren't trying enough! When do you login to work daily?'

'You must fantasize about the customer. Dream about the customer while eating, sleeping, shitting, and brushing. That's how you make a sale in an impossible market. '

'Sell value, not price. Value is permanent, discounts are temporary.'

'Support is the problem? You are the sales-person, you need to provide support to the customers 24x7.'

'I think you have lost your drive. Find your passion and be a go-getter. Seize the world.'

If I had passion, why the heck would I be in this job, I thought to myself. Isn't the lack of passion the reason why we are all here?

On regular days, my shift timing was 2-11 PM. On Month-Ends: the company operated a little differently.

Every shift: Morning, Afternoon, and Night shifts: had to login at 8 AM in the morning and work till 12 PM in the night.

A 16-hour workday.

Every single salesperson from Aspire Solutions would be joining a Google Meet link, circulated among the different Operating Groups the previous day itself through mail and WhatsApp groups.

As the clock struck 8 AM, I grudgingly clicked on the link. I could see multiple people were already joining in the call.

'Hi guys, how are we doing today?' a high pitched and full of irritatingly high energy rang through my earphones.

That was Ajith, the Vice-President of Sales and Marketing at Aspire. His motivational speeches at Month-Ends were supposed to be the stuff of legends. Incidentally, we only heard from him when there was bad news in the company.

'We're doing great, Ajith. Excited to be here in this meeting with you. We are all eager to complete our targets and ensure we hit the milestone stipulated for April,' Abhishek spoke, fawning on Ajith's words.

'Thanks, Abhishek. I am excited to be talking to you guys today. Can we all switch on our cameras please? Let me see your faces, guys!'

Ajith came on camera. There he was, blue supports and black rimmed spectacles, with a clunky smile and slickly gelled black hair, spiked up akin to a raging flame, like he was an early 2000 college kid.

Ninety per cent of the crowd in the call did not switch on their camera, including yours truly. I bet half of them weren't even wearing anything. They had probably joined the call on their phone and were eating breakfast far away in the kitchen.

'Come on, guys. What is this behaviour. Let me see your fresh faces, early in the morning. We have a great day ahead of us. Let's do this!'

Some faces came on-screen. Mostly Ajith's *chamchas*.

'Thank you, team. Now, lets' get down to business.'

'Yes, Ajith. I agree with you completely.' Abhishek smeared some butter.

'Now, you are all aware that today is Month End.'

'No shit.' I murmured.

'I have always looked forward to Month End, it has a similar vibe as a festival does. It's a time to celebrate and have fun.'

There was no response from anyone in the meeting.

'I'm sure many of you have deals in the pipeline, where the customer has agreed to purchase the course, but price is an issue.'

'Make no mistake, I want you all to close those deals today. Talk to your leaders, talk to your business leads for permission on special discounts and get those pots converted by 12 PM tonight.'

I had a few pots I had spoken to Abhishek about, who were asking for more discount than I was authorized to give from my end. This sounded like a great line, I was going to ping Abhishek once again regarding this.

'I understand that a lot of you have been working hard throughout the month to achieve your slabs. Thank you for all your efforts. But today, I want a last push from all of you to help the company achieve its monthly target.'

'Abhishek, what's the Life to Date (LTD) percentage on our monthly target, compared to March?'

Life to Date was the sales we had made from the start of a certain period, say start of the month; till present day.

'We are at 74% LTD as compared to last month, Ajith. I think we can push and over-achieve 110% of the target this month.'

'Dude, what is wrong with this guy? He wants us to keep calling pots till we collapse?' Raman texted in our team group.

'Abhishek's incentive is tied to all of us performing. Obviously, that's the reason for pulling off this stunt in front of everyone.' Soumik pinged.

'Guys, focus on the call, please. We can discuss this later.' Vijay shot off an angry message.

'Yes, boss.'

'I can see that the lead conversion across the Afternoon shift is 15.7 per cent, but Vijay's Operating Group is only at 9.5 per cent. Any insights into that, Vijay?'

Ajith's question had come out of the blue.

To give Vijay credit, his voice was calm and certain.

'Yes Ajith, it's been a tough month for the team, what with most of the leads drying up. We will start hunting on the previous month's pots and close the deals today – giving the customers a month-end discount if need be.'

'Sounds good, Vijay. That's the spirit. This is what I want to hear from you guys.'

'Right now, the time on my computer clock is 8.15 AM. We will be joining the same link every hour from 9 AM onwards. In the next 45 minutes, I want to see some sales getting locked in.'

'Push your pots, negotiate like your life depends on it and get those sales closed.'

'Target the Singapore, Malaysia and Indonesia markets, those pots would already be awake and active by now.'

Ajith sensed that people were listening, but there was absolutely no response to his monologue.

'Abhishek, what do you think? Can we, do it?'

Abhishek did not respond. The whole meeting went silent.

'Abhishek? Are you there?'

'Yes, Ajith...I'm here. Sorry, I was just brushing my...I mean, I was attending to a personal matter.'

'Abhishek, I asked – can we do the target this month? *Hopayega*?'

'Yes Ajith, for sure. We will do it. I will ensure we are on track. Vijay, I need 4 sales from your team by 9 AM. Can we give this assurance to Ajith?'

'Yeah Abhishek, we will get it done.' Vijay replied, in a bored monotone.

'Alright guys, let the games begin! All the very best, Team!' Ajith logged out of the meeting.

Within 30 seconds, I saw another meeting link in our team's WhatsApp group.

It was Vijay. 'Join now, guys. Something important to discuss.'

I wanted to grab a cup of tea before the meeting. I quickly ran to the kitchen, put some hot water in the kettle, and let it boil until the meeting got over.

I clicked on the meeting link Vijay had shared, and adjusted my headsets.

'We're screwed, aren't we?' Raman said.

'Raman, stop talking nonsense. We are behind target as it is, does not mean we cannot put up a good show today.' Vijay switched on his camera.

'Vijay, is this even realistic? We are at LTD revenue of 65% for the month. Now, to achieve the team's target, we need close to 5.45 lakhs in revenue as per the Power BI dashboard. How are we going to do it?'

'Guys, calm down first. Now tell me, what all pots do you have for today? Surya?'

I squirmed in my seat. 'Hi Vijay, I have a few pots for today, will get them converted for sure.'

Vijay was too smart to fall for these works. 'That's great, Surya. Can you be a bit more specific? What is the ticket size of these pots and when can you convert them by?'

'I have to see, Vijay. It's been a tough month and one of the pots was supposed to be a group deal – company sponsored. Now, the company HR has cancelled...'

'Did you not hear my question? I asked, by when can you convert?'

He sounded pissed off. I rephrased my answer.

'Ok, I have two Azure fundamental pots which can be converted. Both are asking for 45% discount. Can I go ahead with this?'

'Granted. I want these two paid before the 9 AM call with Ajith.'

'Umm, no Vijay. The pots will be logging in only by 10 AM. Hopefully, by 12 noon I will get them in.'

'What is the ticket size of the sale?'

'I am aiming for Rs.15.5k-16k per pot.'

'Give the course at Rs.14k and drop in a free self-paced course. I want both the pots converted before 9 AM. What else?'

'Ok, thanks Vijay. I will call them now. I have another Python for Data Science course, which I am trying to convert at full price. The pot says he is not too interested in a discount, since the amount is reimbursed by the company.'

'He is pushing to pay next month, though. It seems, his salary will come only the 5th of the next month.'

'Isn't this guy a Senior Analyst at Google? These people earn a ton. Do one thing, upsell him to a Python Masters course and drop in some free Aspire Learning credits. You are authorized to sell the course till Rs.45k, not below this.'

'But, Vijay – I have spoken to this guy. He will pay, just that he doesn't have the full cash with him until the salary date.'

'What kind of salesperson are you anyway? Make up some stories and get this pot paid by 4 PM today. Hard sell an EMI option to this guy and ensure he makes the first downpayment by evening.'

'Okay, Vijay. I will do this. Hopefully, if I get this done – I will achieve my slab.'

'Yeah, tough luck buddy. You will your Slab 1, IF – and that's a big IF, you convert that Python course to a Python Masters.

I felt a bead of sweat on my forehead.

'Yes, Vijay. Understood.'

CHAPTER TEN

MONTH END-MOTIVATION AND MAYHEM-PART 2

'What is the plan, people? Are we going to do achieve our targets, or not?'

The beaming smile was gone. It was replaced by an angry looking, bespectacled human.

Ajith was fuming. It was already 6 PM. We had met every 1 hour from 9 AM onwards, but the results were not promising. Each Group was making multiple calls to customers, referrals, and their relatives.

To top it all, 30th April fell on a Monday – which meant that working professionals were not very likely to answer to any discounts, forget sales calls.

I was half-sleepy, and could hardly keep myself awake. Would the World collapse if we didn't do our targets?

'Abhishek, what the hell is happening? Are you in control of the situation or not?'

Abhishek whimpered. He could see his promotion to Senior Business Manager flutter away in the wind.

'Yes, yes...Ajith. We are, I mean, the team is trying hard to get the pots converted. It's just that this is a weekday, and that too a Monday. So, it's a little hard to get people to pay...'

'Abhishek, Abhishek. Listen to me. And listen to me, clearly. I don't care. I don't care what excuses you guys are going to come up with.'

'Did I not mention that at the start of every month, you need to push your pots to pay? By the 15th of the month, you would be at 70% of target and by the 25th – you will be done with your target? Did I not say this?'

'Abhishek is right, Ajith. This is a tough day to crack. Right now, all the pots would be logging off from work. We will get them converted in the next two hours.'

That was Ravi, head of business for the Morning shift.

'Ravi, your team is pathetically behind target. Morning shift is at 67% LTD. Any comments?'

'We'll get it done, Ajith.'

'You better. The higher-ups are after my life to get the targets done, and you guys are here laying eggs, waiting for them to hatch.'

'Right now, the sales team is at 86% LTD for the month. We will not aim for achieving 110% target. Instead, we will attempt 100% for this month.'

'But Ajith, 110% is doable, let's aim high...' Abhishek started to apply butter.

'Please, Abhishek. I have heard enough. Team, I hope you were paying attention.'

'We will now meet again by 8 PM. Beg, borrow, steal – do whatever you want. Like Ravi mentioned, the pots have now logged off from work and would be active on WhatsApp, call, and mail. Ensure that you are getting connects and close the deals.'

'I will await good news. Only good news, mind you.'

I yawned loudly. Unfortunately, my microphone was on in the meet.

'What the...who was that? Who is that person? Is this a joke?' Ajith screamed.

I immediately muted my microphone.

Luckily, Ajith's internet connection seems to have conked off as he abruptly left the meeting. I heaved a sigh of relief.

'Dude, Surya. That was close, man. Never do that again.' Raman pinged me on WhatsApp.

'Bhai, I logged off today morning at 1 AM, logging in again for the stupid morning call at 8 AM. What do I do?'

'Chill, chill. Don't worry about it. We are all in the same boat.'

My phone pinged once again. This time, it was Vijay.

'Team, join the link I have shared now. Be quick, we need to get back to calling.'

I saw Raman and Soumik already in the call. Vijay was yet to join.

'Hi guys, did you make any sales today?' I asked.

'I closed 2 pots. One was for an Amazon Web Services for 15.5k, and the other for Cybersecurity Essentials at full price,' Raman said.

'Damn, that's good. Soumik bhai, how about you?'

'Made only one sale, Surya. Vijay will give *bamboo* now.'

Vijay joined the call as Soumik was talking.

'I am not going to bullshit here, team. We are behind target and you know that. Raman, are you only going to get 2 sales today? What happened to the PMP pot?'

'Vijay...I'm already done with my Slab 1. Right now, Slab 2 is impossible as I need to cover 8 lakhs. So...,' Raman dragged on.

'Yeah? So what? Remember you are part of a team and we aren't talking about your individual achievements. Only if the team achieves the month's target, I make money.'

'Yes, Vijay. I understand. We will get it done.'

'Surya Sir, any updates? Only one sale?'

I had got that one sale by literally pleading with the customer. The guy was smart, he understood that I was desperate to make my slab and manipulated me to selling the course to him at 11k, a full three thousand below the limit Vijay had set for me.

The Masters guy wasn't responding to me, nor on call or text.

'I'm trying, Vijay. The other guy for Azure is having some issues in payment since his credit card isn't working for the EMI option.'

'Is he for real? Tell me to pay the full amount right now. Give 2 self-paced courses free.'

'I'm working on it. He is calling his sister for her card, hopefully it should come through today.'

'Fine. Even then, you seem to be below the target for this month.'

'So, you have a sale for 11k. Let's leave that. Assuming, that you make the 14k sale to the customer, you still need about 40k in revenue to achieve your target this month. I hope you know that revenue calculation does not include the 18% GST.'

Shit, this guy was fast.

'Which means that, you either make three sales at a good ticket price in the next six hours, or else get that Masters guy to pay before midnight.'

Vijay had put me in a spot.

'Vijay, I was just thinking – what if Raman gives....'

'Gives you his revenue to complete your target? In your dreams.' Vijay completed my sentence.

'Just because Raman cannot make his Slab 2, doesn't mean I will transfer his excess Slab 1 revenue to you for target completion. If you want your incentive, get it done by yourself.'

'Sure, Vijay. Thank you.' I said with gritted teeth.

Soumik was grilled as well, but since he had 2-3 sure shots in the line, he was left off the hook. I, on the other, was right in the line of fire.

'Thank you, team, you may leave the call. We will regroup on the main link at 8 PM sharp. Surya, your time starts now.'

I exited the call, took off my head-phones, and slammed it against my door.

How was all this my fault? The market was down, companies were downsizing and pots were not returning my calls or messages.

What was I to do?

I shut my laptop and decided to go down for a walk. 'I need some fresh air to clear my mind,' I said to myself.

It was nice to walk outside, away from my laptop. It was already late evening, the Sun setting over the horizon. The sky was a blend of red and orange shades overlapping with each other. I saw a few kids playing with a football, running, and chasing each other in abandon.

'Ah, what a life. No pressure to earn money at this age. Just go to school, learn History we will never use in our entire life and then come home to sleep.'

'...jghk!!'

'I wish I could go back to those days. I miss watching cartoons.'

'...rya!'

'What if I just quit my job? What if I just sat at home, ate ice-cream and binge watched TV shows online. I'll find another job, Let me put in my papers today, I'll show Vijay what I can do. Abhishek can stuff his face with my resignation letter....'

'Surya! How many times do I call you?' I heard a voice behind me.

I turned around in irritation. Who the heck was this person? I was having a life crisis to deal with, and from nowhere a voice comes from the Heavens to be answered.

I turned around to find out the source of the voice.

Just my good luck. It was Shekhar, one of my classmates from school.

Shekhar was one of those guys who loved poking his nose into other's business, whether it involved him in the least, or not. He was the type of guy who would not shy away from asking you anything under the Sun, regarded as personal – salary, bank balance, dating life situationships and much more.

Shekhar knew more about me than even Google did, and that's saying something.

'Surya, hi. I saw you walking around the park briskly and called out to you. Busy day, is it?'

'Yeah, hi Shekhar. As you know, today is...'

'Month end, right? Yes, of course. You're done with your target?'

'Yes...I mean, no...I'm in the process of...'

'*Acha*, so you haven't completed your Slab 1? Man, life is tough. Then, no incentive this month for you. How are you going to pay your phone's EMI, bro?'

I clenched my fist in anger.

'Shekhar, how is work? Did you get that promotion you were waiting for?'

Shekhar's expression changed. Somehow, his own medicine wasn't as sweet anymore.

'Surya, I have to go the gym right now. I have been trying to bulk up my body since some time. I will see you later. Bye,' Shekhar turned around abruptly and began to walk away.

Wait, what did he just say?

'Shekhar, wait! Aye, idiot. Wait, man.'

'Hey Surya, did you just call me an idiot?'

'What is the use? Only then will you respond to me. Listen, what was the last line you said to me before leaving?'

'I am unable to understand.' Shekhar scratched his head.

'You said something about going to the gym?' I prompted.

'Hmm...yes, correct. I have to go to the gym. It's time I started to bulk up my body. How else will I get a girlfriend?'

My brain sparked with an idea. Why did I not think of this before? Really, Vijay was right. I was a hopeless salesperson.

'Thanks, Shekhar! I owe you one. Bye, bye!' I started to run in the direction of my house.

'Hey! Tell me if you achieve your target and get a raise! I want to know how much is your revised salary.' I heard Shekhar's voice masked by the honking of a Tempo traveller behind me.

Genuis, just genius. This was a classic month end tactic, and here I was – completely out of the game.

Suddenly, my phone rang.

'Hi Surya! This is Karthik, remember we were speaking about the Azure course.'

'Can you send me the link right away? I will do the payment now.'

My brain went into a freeze. Was this really happening?

'Hi Karthik, I am away from my laptop right now. Can I share you the payment link in another 15 minutes?' I said.

The silence on the other side of the line was deafening.

'Is it? I am leaving for a family dinner right now. It's not urgent, then. Let's complete the deal next week and you can help me with the enrolment. Bye, now.'

'Karthik, wait!'

Again, silence. This time, I was going to drive the conversation.

'I will share you the payment link on mail and WhatsApp right now. It will be via our partner payment gateway. Once the payment is done, I will send you the login credentials for your course. Does that sound good?'

'All that is fine, Surya. I am using my sister's card, and we are in a hurry. Can we finish this process quickly?'

'Yes, yes, of course. I'll call you back in two minutes. Please keep your card details ready.'

I hung up the call. In a flash, I opened my team's WhatsApp group.

'Guys, I have a payment. Need a link.' I pinged.

'Yes, boss. Available and ready. Ping the details.' Raman responded.

'Azure Cloud Fundamentals at 14k inclusive of GST, no cost EMI for credit card.'

'Email id is _karthik_cloudprof21@gmail.com_. Select the 18th May, Week-End batch.'

'Keep the link validity for 15 minutes.' I concluded.

'Which bank?' Raman pinged.

Our company offered customers different options while paying using credit cards. Depending on the interest rates offered as well as the ease of payment coming through to us, we salespersons recommended a bank's name from the drop-down list in our system.

'Select HDFC Credit card, 3 months No Cost EMI.'

'Ok, done. Sending the link now. I am populating his other details from the CRM. Ask him to check his mail and WhatsApp.'

I pinged Karthik. 'Hi Karthik, you would have received a payment link from my colleague, Raman. Can you proceed with the payment now?'

'Yes, I have received now. I will update you once the payment is done.'

'Thanks, Karthik. Keep me updated in case any issue arises.' I pinged.

Typically, the sales team knew exactly where a customer was during the payment process for a course – right from the point when they touched the link to the point when the payment was done.

The backend systems used the following nomenclature:

a. TL: Touched Link. It means that the customer has accessed the landing page of the payment link, typically where the course fee and the item being purchased are displayed.
b. GTP: Going to Pay. The customer has gone past the landing page and is entering her/his bank details.
c. FP: Final Payment. The customer is giving a final confirmation to the payment gateway to debit the amount from the customer's bank account.

Once the payment was done, I would receive an email notification stating 'Payment Received.' Then, I would share the login credentials and onboarding instructions related to their specific batch.

Right now, I had a problem.

I could see that Karthik had immediately clicked on the link, gone in a flash from TL to GTP.

He had not reached the FP stage yet. Already, 10 minutes had gone by.

'Is he going to pay?' Vijay pinged in the group.

'Yes, Vijay. He is having some bank issues. I will check with him and let you know.' I bluffed, confidently.

I called up Karthik. The line kept ringing; he wasn't picking up.

Two more minutes passed. The payment link was going to expire in the next 180 seconds.

Getting a payment link unpaid was akin to getting a one-way ticket to Hell. It showed that you could not judge a customer's intention to pay – which was the worst insult you could give a sales agent. An unpaid link meant having Ajith, Abhishek, and Vijay in one meeting. I shuddered at the thought.

I kept calling Karthik. There was only one minute to go.

He still wasn't picking up. What was with this guy?

I clasped my face in my hands. 'I am going to quit, I am done with this job.'

'Maybe I will retire and go to the Himalayas.'

Forget it, flight tickets to the Himalayas are too expensive. Inflation just kills salvation.

My computer pinged.

'Paid. Congrats, Surya. One more payment and target is done for this month.' Raman pinged.

Paid? How come?

My phone started to buzz angrily. It was Karthik.

'Hey, Surya. Sorry man, the payment was delayed. There were no bank issues this time. I had a slight case of err...loose motion.'

'I was in the process of doing the payment, when I had to rush to the toilet. I think the payment is done from my end; can you confirm?'

I checked the CRM for Karthik's ID. Indeed, the payment had come through.

'Thanks Karthik, for your business. I am sharing the login credentials for the course with you. Until the course starts on 18th May, there are some pre-uploaded lectures and course material you can go through until then.'

'Let me know if you have any questions.'

'Sure, Surya. Thanks again. Appreciate your help.' Karthik hung up.

I breathed a sigh of relief.

Not yet, though. It was already 8 PM. I was still way off to achieving my target.

Would I make it, this month?

CHAPTER ELEVEN

MONTH END-MOTIVATION AND MAYHEM-PART 3

I joined the main link. Ajith was already in the call.

He seemed relaxed. Something was off.

'So, hello team. Hope you are doing well. Abhishek? All good?'

'Ajith Sir, of course; things are always good, with you running the sales team.'

'Thank you, Abhishek. Looks like a major part of the team has joined the call.'

'Without wasting further time, let us begin.'

He pulled up a Power BI dashboard on the screen. I squinted my eyes to look at the data more clearly. There were numerous charts and numbers running across the dashboard, that I lost interest immediately.

'Well, as you can see – the data tells us a story. The entire sales team is now at 94% LTD for April, as compared to last month. Guys, congratulations. This is a great achievement, and you all deserve a pat on your backs for this.'

This was Ajith's style. First flatter the prey, then go for the kill.

'But we are not done yet. The team is very close to the 100% LTD target. Let's give that final push today and ensure that we get the revenue rolling in.'

'Can we do it guys? Are you with me?'

'Yes, Ajith.' A few *chamchas* echoed.

'I'd like to recognize Vijay and team here, as well. I gave Vijay a hard time during the previous meetings, and it seems like he has really gone supersonic in getting those payments in. Well done Vijay and team, keep up the good work.'

'Thanks Ajith.' Vijay said happily.

'That's it from my side, guys. Have your dinner, ensure that we get those payments rolling and those unpaid links sent out, paid. Chase the pots as if this was your last day and close the deals.'

'The Indian market will be active for a maximum of three hours now, till 11 PM that is. Start calling your US pots as well and close them with a month end deal. Talk to your team leads in case you need any special permission with regards to offers.'

'All the best. Bye, now.' Ajith exited the call.

'That wasn't a bad meeting,' I thought to myself. 'The only problem being, I am going to be the only guy in the team who will not get his target done.'

Like a voice from the Heavens, Vijay pinged me personally.

'What happened to that Masters payment?'

I had forgotten about that entirely.

'He isn't responding to me. I will try again and update you.' I pinged back, then slammed my phone onto my bed.

I went to my CRM homepage, and immediately created a report of the pots which had not been closed in the last quarter, but had shown adequate interest in our courses. I applied a filter for years of experience, course type and activity done on the website. Just for namesake, I filtered for India, US, and UK pots. Who knew, I might get lucky tonight.

Around 500 results popped up. 'This was good enough.' I said to myself.

I copied all the email ids from the report and pasted them into a mail template Raman had sent me last month. I wondered how I had missed executing such a critical action, that too on a month end.

When nothing worked, this did. The Brahmastra of sales.

Bulk mailers. That was what Shekhar had reminded me of when he mentioned his gym schedule.

I clicked 'Send.' Done.

Now, All I had to do was wait.

I picked up my phone and called Vijay. 'Hi Vijay, I've sent out a bulk mailer with our Month End Deal.'

'20% off plus 20% cashback on all courses. Hopefully, something should work out.'

There was a pause.

'Ok, good. Remember, you have only three and a half hours to get your Masters payments to cover your remaining target of 40k.'

'Or, if you have plans to get in three singular course payments, that works for me as well.'

'Understood, Vijay. Thanks for reminding me.' I replied, acidly.

I shut my laptop once again. The time was now 8.30 PM.

'Let me have dinner and take a quick nap, what was the worst that could happen?'

'If the payment comes, it comes. It doesn't come – well, too bad. I will apply butter on Abhishek.'

I ensured that I stuffed myself with dinner, before dozing off on my couch, with my laptop screen active.

It wasn't clear how long I was asleep – but I do know for a fact that someone had splashed water on my face as I was dreaming about playing cricket with Sachin Tendulkar. For some reason, he was trying to sell me a life insurance policy. I wondered if he had insurance against PIPs as well.

'Here, try this life insurance policy. The benefits are great,' Sachin said.

'Sachin, bowl one over at least. We will see all this later.'

'Surya, take the policy – you will not regret it. It has insurance against Abhishek as well.'

'Oh, really? I will take it then. Bowl one over to me, first. Trial ball, then reals.'

In place of a cricket ball, Sachin threw a water balloon at my face; the balloon spinning in a vicious manner. As I tried to swing my bat to make contact with the balloon, I missed it hopelessly and felt the balloon make contact with my face instead.

'Idiot! Get up, right now! How many times do I have to call you?'

'Sachin, *yaar* – what language is this? I will complain to BCCI...'

'Who Sachin? Do I look like Sachin?'

I rubbed my eyes. It was my brother, standing at the edge of the couch upon which I had dozed off.

'Your laptop has been pinging continuously since the time you knocked yourself out. Someone called 'Pranjal Customer' has given you five missed calls,' my brother said.

I felt a bolt of lightning go through my body.

'That must be from the bulk mailer I sent out.'

I checked the time. Shit, it was 11.30 PM. Half an hour before the showdown, thirty minutes to decide if I were to do my target this month or not.

I checked the team chat on my laptop. Raman has pinged me; Vijay had pinged me; Soumik had pinged me. They were all saying the same thing.

'CHECK YOUR MAIL!!!'

I flipped open my Gmail Inbox. And there it was.

Pranjal, one of my old customers who had given me a hard time before deciding not to buy any course from me, had replied to my bulk mailers email. It ran as follows:

'Hi Surya, hope you are doing well.'

'I can see the course fee for Devops Certification on the Aspire website is Rs.17,995. When I am trying to pay, it showing a total of Rs.21,234.'

'I am interested in this deal mentioned in the email. Instead of 20% off, which comes to around 16.9k, can we go ahead at a flat price of 16k for the Devops Certification course? It is 3 people in total looking to enrol for the May 4th, Weekend batch.'

'I tried calling you multiple times, it seems to me that you are busy. Let me know if I can go ahead with the enrolment.'

I glanced at the chat windows on the left side of my screen. Vijay's abuses and anger at my utter desecration of the ethos of a Month End, by snoring peacefully when three major sales were about to slip out of my hands – are not literature friendly and cannot be reproduced here.

I snapped up my phone and returned Pranjal's number.

'Hi Pranjal! How are you? Yes, I'm good thank you. Yes, about that...I was in the middle of a family emergency and didn't see your call. You'll enrol later? No, that's not necessary, we can go ahead now, I won't be able to hold the offer till tomorrow...you know, Month Ends and managers...ha ha ha.'

'What about your family emergency? Please take care, all this can wait. Family is important, Surya,' Pranjal said in a worried tone.

'Pranjal, if you don't enrol today – trust me, I will be in the ICU.'

'What?'

'So, would you be available to proceed with the payment right now?' I switched the topic of discussion.

'Yes, we can go ahead with the deal. Only if, the price is at 16k per person.'

'I was just on call with my manager. Since you have already shown interest in the Devops course before, I have got special permission to ensure that this deal is available to you at the mentioned price. Hope this is satisfactory to you.'

'Sounds good to me. I am sharing my details and my colleagues' details for the enrolment. I want the 20% cashback as mentioned in the mail as well.'

'No worries, I will ensure it is credited to your digital wallet.'

I pinged Raman. 'Raman bhai, ready?'

'Yes, Sir. Send me the details.'

Within the next sixty seconds, Pranjal and his two friends had enrolled for the Devops course at the agreed upon price.

Suddenly, I got a ping on my phone.

It was a US number. Funny, I didn't have any outstanding US pots. Who was pinging me now?

I opened the message. It ran as follows:

'Hey Surya, Chris here from Florida. I received your contact from a friend of mine who enrolled in an Azure

Master program with you a few months back. He absolutely loved the course and the support you've provided him.'

'I'd like to go ahead with the same course as well in the upcoming batch. Can you enrol me in right away at 850 USD? I can complete the payment in instalments if we can agree at the final price.'

Holy shit, was this my lucky, lucky day? How things turn around so quickly. I pinged Vijay in my excitement.

'Vijay, listen. I have a US payment coming through right now.'

He pinged back. 'How much?'

'850 USD. Should I send him the link?'

There was a pause.

I pinged back. 'Vijay, there?'

The typing sign came up against his name.

'Do not take his payment now. Ask Raman to send him a link tomorrow for the payment. Make up some bullshit about tech issues, and the payment will go through tomorrow only, post-midnight India time.'

I was flabbergasted. Why would Vijay not take a payment landing right into my lap? It was a Masters payment, and a US one at that. The revenue generated from this one payment would be close to 70,000 in INR.

Vijay understood, and pinged again. 'I will explain. Do as I say.'

Every inch of my body resisted Vijay's words. But, end of the day – he was the boss. I pinged the US customer stating some payment issues had come through at our end, we would send out the link in the next 30 minutes.

'Yep cool, makes sense. Let me know when your systems are ready to go,' Chris pinged back.

I glanced at the clock.

It was 11.59 PM.

Did I do my target? I don't know. In fact, I was too tired to think about anything.

My phone buzzed. It was Vijay.

Before he could speak, I started talking. 'Vijay, look man. I'm sorry the target didn't happen this month. Next month, for sure I will do it. Please don't kick me out...'

'Can you shut up for one second? Let me ask you this. Did you really pass your maths exams in school, or not?'

'What do you mean?' I asked, bewildered.

'You sold 3 courses at the rate of 16k each. First off, damn good ticket size. Second of all, you generated revenue of 40.7k in a matter of 20 minutes.'

'Okay...' I could see where this was going.

'Which means, you are done with your slab for the month. Congratulations. Well done, once again.'

Wow. I did not see that coming. It was a moment to celebrate, for sure.

'Thanks, Vijay. I'm sorry about not seeing the calls till the last minute...'

'Listen to me, Surya. We are all human beings. I know how hard you guys have been working this month, but it is my job to ensure that we get the targets done, no matter what. I have always told you, follow the process and the results will follow.'

'You did just that this month, which is why you deserve it.'

'Hmm, thanks Vijay. Appreciate it.' I nodded my head.

'Also, I would have given you Raman's revenue in case if you didn't CLOSE those 3 sales.'

'Really, you would do for me?'

'Yeah, I had already discussed this with the team. You were close, but not too close. Wanted to see how far you could push yourself. Seems like some good came out the pressure, then.'

I didn't know whether to thank him or smash his face into a wall the next time I had a chance to meet him. All that came out of my mouth was:

'Thanks, Vijay. Your wisdom is so profound. Come, let us join the final link for the Month End results call at 12 AM,' I cooed, sweetly.

'Yeah, let's do it. Ajith is barking already, asking everyone to join.' Vijay cut the call.

I checked the time on my computer. It was 12 AM.

The end of a month. The start of another.

I clicked on the master link to join in. Ajith had a very neutral expression on his face Abhishek was having a very disinterested look. Really, this is what I joined the link for? I could have revisited my decision and gone to sleep instead.

'Raman bhai, what's happening? Did the company do the target this time or not?' I pinged.

'No idea, bro. Everyone's lips are sealed. Even I am waiting for the film climax.'

'Yeah, some picture these guys have been showing us since the beginning. Ok, let's wait.'

Ajith's voice cut through our conversation.

'Ok, everyone's here? Ravi, please ask the Night shift guys to join in as well. They can get back to calling in about 15 minutes, maximum. I understand everyone's tired.'

'Sure, Ajith. I'll send the message across,' Ravi said.

'Thanks. Abhishek, can you share your screen? I believe we have the month's results come through.' Ajith said.

'Yes, sure Ajith, I am pulling it up now...yes, I'm up. Can everyone see my screen?'

'Yes, Abhishek. It's visible.'

'So, guys, here we have the results for this month. At a company level, we have achieved 104% of our LTD target, which is quite impressive seeing where we were today morning.'

'Is it really? Abhishek, do you think so?' Ajith sneered.

'Yes...I mean, no. No, not at all, it's a terrible score. We should be doing 150% of our target every month, that is the objective...' Abhishek stammered.

'Good. Continue, please.'

'Well, yes...from the dashboard – morning shift has done 81% of the target, afternoon shift has done 110% of the target and night shift has....'

'Yes, thank you. I can see the data. Let's move on now.'

'So, it's clear that Morning Shift and the Night shift have lagged behind in their sales. Ravi and Nakul, any comments?'

Nakul was the head of the Night shift.

'Hi Ajith, Ravi here. Nakul is on a customer call, so he couldn't be here.'

'This month wasn't great for the Morning shift. It seems like a lot of pots have been deferring their payments due to cost restructuring and new company policies.'

'Wonderful. Then how did the Afternoon shift do their target?'

There was no response from Ravi.

'Well, they are targeting the same companies, same people – having to deal with the same company policies, isn't it? '

'Ajith, I...'

'Ravi, it means that your salespeople are not trained well enough. We will have a one-on-one call soon to discuss the future plans of the morning shift.'

'Sure, Ajith.' Ravi muted himself.

'As for the Night shift, Nakul and I will have an alternate conversation all together. His team has done abysmally bad this month. Afternoon shift has emerged as the saviour this month. Good job, Abhishek.'

Abhishek's cheeks glowed with happiness as his eyes filled with tears. 'Good job, Afternoon shift. Let's continue this performance next month as well.'

'Yes, please do. Now, let's move on to the star performers for the month, shall we?'

A slide was pulled up. Right there, at the bottom right I noticed my name etched in white font against a blood red background.

'Surya – Slab 1 achieved.'

The team group flooded with congratulations. It felt great, but tiring as well. 'This entire circus of achieving the target this month has had few highs, many lows. Will I make it to this list, again next month?'

Vijay pinged me. 'Send the payment link to the US guy and close him now.'

'Sure, I'll do that,' I clicked on the payment link generator and punched in the details. That's when I realized what Vijay was talking about. He truly was a genius.

Getting in revenue of 70k this month would be of no use to me, I would never have achieved Slab 2, since I would be off my target by a few lakhs. But now, by getting a link paid post 12 AM, I would have started the first day of the next month with a revenue worth 70k. Smart guy, Vijay was.

Two days later, I logged into the daily sales team meeting call.

Abhishek and Vijay were waiting, along with Raman and Soumik.

'Hi Surya, why are you on zero? Any sure shots for today?' Abhishek asked.

'But I got a US payment yesterday,' I protested.

'That was yesterday, what about today? Your Dad will get the payment for you?'

And, the cycle continues.

You are always as good as yesterday, right?

CHAPTER TWELVE

IT'S A DEAL, AND A DATE!

'Ma'am, please try and understand. This is the best deal you are going to get.' I haggled.

'Surya, listen to me. I am not going to pay one penny more than 14k. It's my final offer. I'm ready to postpone this deal to even 2 months later. It's really up to you whether you want to make the sale right now, or not.'

Shikhara was a tough customer. She was aiming for the Kubernetes course at a highly discounted price, while I was aiming to achieve my target for the day.

'Ma'am, can we come to a middle ground?'

'Really? And what is that?'

'Just give me a second, I am trying to work something out.' I bought myself some time.

I looked through her LinkedIn profile to present her a lucrative offer.

'Hmm...experience with networking, storage, computer architecture. Three years of experience in the IT field and...wait, what's this?'

Something interesting lay waiting in her education details.

'KPY School, Batch of 2016?' I said aloud.

'Sorry, what's that?'

'I mean, Ma'am...Shikhara, you're from KPY School?'

'Yeah, so what?'

'You're from the 2016 batch? Karun's batch?'

There was a minute of silence on the other line.

'How do you...who are you, again?' Shikhara asked. The tension was palpable in her voice.

'Shikhara, it's Surya, remember? We had worked together in the Prime Minister's Conclave event. I was the co-head of the event with Sharan?'

'Ohh! Now I remember! You're that Surya...how are you? What are you up to nowadays?'

Shikhara has been my junior during my school days. As seniors in the 12th grade, we had undertaken the responsibility of inducting the juniors on the intricacies of conducting a National Level event in our school, along the lines of a Model United Nations.

'He he, I'm into sales right now – as is visible currently.' I gestured to no one in particular at the obvious.

'Right, yes – sorry, that was a dumb question. Wow, has it been that long back? It just seems like yesterday.'

'Yeah, you still look as pretty as you did back in school.' I said aloud, looking at her profile photo.

Shit, that was supposed to be in my head. Why the heck would I say something like that on a recorded call?

There was a giggle on the other side of the line. 'Well, someone remembers a few things about me, then.'

'Shikhara, my bad. It wasn't supposed to come out the way it did, and I...'

'Oh? So, you didn't mean what you said, is it?'

I was trapped. Time to squirm out of the situation.

'So, coming back to our point of discussion. We can close the deal at a final price of 15k flat, inclusive of GST. Along with this, you will be getting...,' Shikhara cut me off.

'Listen, mister. I am not interested in this deal. I will pay the full price as per the website.'

'You would do that?' I felt stupid. What was the need of haggling all this time then?

'Yes. But you have to explain the statement you said earlier. This is my condition.'

'Else, you can forget about the deal. I have 3 more of my friends who want to enrol; I will tell them explicitly, not to choose Aspire.'

'Shikhara, are you blackmailing me?'

'Take it as you like. It's really up to you.'

'I will call your bluff. There are no 3 friends who want to enrol. If that was the case, you would have told me about this earlier in the call and negotiated a better deal.'

'Toss a coin, take a chance. Why do I care? All I'm asking is a simple answer.'

I was now hanging between the Devil and the Deep Sea. Should I tell her everything? Or risk losing 3 potential sales?

Abhishek's face came to the forefront. I made my decision immediately.

'Right, ahem. So, as I saying...' I began.

'You were in the hospitality part of the event; I was in the public relations and administration vertical. Ramesh...Prem! Yes, Prem. I remember telling Prem that there was this girl called Shikhara, she looked cute.'

'That's it. Nothing else. Can we proceed with the deal?' I concluded.

I could hear stifled laughter on the other end of the line.

'Ok, after that?'

'What do you mean '*after that*'? Nothing.' I said.

'Really? Pallavi has told me another story. Or, should I refresh your memory?'

My entire world came crashing down. Pallavi was my classmate and supposedly, close friend. Did people not understand the concept of a secret?

I felt now would be a good time to reveal everything.

'Yeah, I had mentioned to Pallavi about you, checking with her if you were in a relationship.'

'She said yes. So, I didn't pursue the topic any further.'

'That's interesting. At the time of the event, I wasn't in a relationship. I wonder why Pallavi would say something like that.'

'Forget Pallavi, why didn't you come and ask me out directly?' Shikhara said.

'I...I don't know. I really don't know. Can we change the topic?' I was ready to forgo this sale, this was not worth it.

'You can ask me now, you know,' she said. The pause after her voice was pregnant with tension.

I twiddled with the pencil on my desk.

'Right, sure. Can we go ahead with the group deal?' I asked.

'No, silly...God, you boys are just so...Surya, listen. Why don't you ask me now?'

'Ask you what?'

'Do you want to...y'know?' she said, her voice trailing away.

'Do I want to, what?' I really wasn't getting it.

'Man, I knew boys were a little slow – but this slow, God help him.'

Shikhara took a deep breath.

'Surya, will you go out with me for a cup of coffee?'

I was sitting at the edge of my chair, with the back-legs of the chair hanging in mid-air. The moment I heard Shikhara's words, I lost my balance in utter surprise, as my body slammed the floor.

'Hello, hello? Surya, are you there? I heard a lot of noise at your end. Did you fall of your chair or something?'

My headphones had come loose, along with my sanity. I regained my composure and fixed my headphones back on.

'Cup of coffee? Really, you want to go on a date?'

Now, it was her time to squirm.

'Dude, don't make me repeat it again. This is really awkward.' she laughed, nervously.

'I did have a crush on you back then, y'know. I told Pallavi, also. Looks like she didn't convey my message to you as well,' she sighed.

Aha. Pallavi seemed to be the common villain in this interesting triangle. I would talk to Pallavi later on about her intentions.

'That's interesting. Hey, now let me turn the tables on you. Why didn't you ask me out directly then? We used to sit just two tables away during the event,' I asked.

'Well, yeah – there is an unwritten rule that girls would never ask a guy out.'

'Also, you seemed like a guy who was very serious about studies and life. I thought you might say no, so I didn't bother to pursue. I thought, maybe Pallavi could tell you about me and something could have happened.'

'But hey, whatever happened, happened for good! Who knew we would meet like this on call today? Such an unusual situation, no?'

I couldn't agree more.

'So...let's meet up when you're free?' Shikhara said, expectantly.

'Yeah, sure. Let's catch up on a date. This is what it is, right?' I asked, half-joking.

'Well, you can call it whatever you like. At least this time, let's ensure that there isn't any third party involved here.'

'That's hilarious. Yes, I completely agree.'

There was a pause. I decided to break the ice.

'Let's do one thing, Shikhara. I'll give you the course at 14k flat. It was nice catching up with you today.'

'You know what, Surya? I was having a really bad day today, until this phone call. Now, my mood has really improved.'

'I am right now on your company website. I am going to pay the full price for the course, no discounts. Those 3 enrolments? I wasn't bluffing. I will ensure that they enrol with you only.'

'Shikhara, you don't have to...' I started.

'One second, mister. I'm not done. I am not doing this as a charity. The dates that we are going to go on? You're paying.'

'I'm sorry, I thought it was only one date. Did you say *dates*, as in plural? As in, multiple *dates*?'

'I am cutting the call now, Surya. Bye. Enjoy your day.' I knew she had turned red.

Two days later, Vijay rang me up.

'Hi, Surya. How are you doing today?'

'I'm good, Vijay. Don't worry, today's daily target will be done. I have 2 pots ready to pay in the next one hour.'

'That's all fine. How was your date?'

I froze. 'What date, Vijay?'

'The one you were going to go with Shikhara, the Kubernetes pot?'

'Umm...yeah, wait – how do you know about her?'

'She paid full price, also. I haven't seen anyone pay full price for Kubernetes.'

'Vijay, how do you know about Shikhara?' I asked again.

'Idiot, this is my job. If I didn't know what was happening with my team, what kind of Team Lead would I be?'

I gave a sheepish smile.

'I have the call recording with me. Next time you want to do romance, do it from your personal phone, no?'

'Sure, Vijay. I will make a note of this for future reference.' I said, sarcastically.

'You better, lover boy. I want those 3 enrolments closed by the end of this week, as mentioned in the conversation. Or else, this call recording goes straight to

Ajith and Abhishek directly. You can explain how you have used company money for your romantic escapades.'

Romance can come in any form, size, or shape.

Anti-romance, on the other hand – take the form of pesky Team Leads.

CHAPTER THIRTEEN

PUT IT ON EMAIL

'Surya, check your lead assignment. Kiran George is back.' Prem pinged me.

'Sorry, who?' I asked.

'Kiran George, dude. He is famous all over Aspire for never having spoken to a single salesperson here. He purchases courses only via email.'

'How can someone purchase a course only based on email communication? He must have spoken to someone, for advice or discounts.' I argued.

'No, that has never been the case. Make sure you deal with him carefully. All the best.'

'Heh, amateurs. I'll make sure I get him on call, otherwise he won't be purchasing any course from me.' It was a battle of egos now.

I checked Kiran's details in my system. *'kirangeorgemail@gmail.com.'*

Hmm, his mail id has a 'mail' in it. Interesting character. There was no phone number provided. He had shown interest in the 'Generative AI Essentials' course on our website. There was no request for a callback, only a small message.

'Hi, this is Kiran George. I am a software professional with over 20 years of experience in the field of Information Technology. As you may be aware, I have purchased multiple courses from Aspire in the past, and am currently looking forward to pursue the 'Generative AI Essentials' course from your platform.'

'The batch I am looking to enrol in is on May 1st, Weekend batch. I am willing to enrol at the final price of Rs.17,000.'

'If interested in this deal, kindly revert via the email id provided, I can proceed with the payment with my corporate credit card. Thanks.'

I ran through the email two times. And then, a third time.

Typically, this is known as a 'sure-shot'- in sales parlance. It means that the probability of a sale coming through is 100%.

Right now, only Prem knew about the lead assignment. The rest of the team was busy and Vijay was on leave. I decided to take a risk and strike a Deal with the Devil. At this point of the month, I was already ahead of my LTD target. If I didn't take risks, what kind of salesperson would I be?

If I didn't make another stupid decision, how could I justify my salary?

I opened up my mailbox, typing in the following email to Kiran:

'Hi Kiran, thank you for your interest in the Generative AI course.'

'I am glad to know that you have dropped a message to us, displaying your keen interest in our courses. It is heartening to see that you have been a regular learner with us throughout your professional journey.'

'Please find attached the course curriculum, for your reference. Along with this, I am attaching a sample recording of the course – which can be viewed at your leisure and convenience.'

'I would be happy to walk you through the course features and what we at Aspire can offer to make your learning experience more enriching and fruitful. Do let me a convenient time to connect with you, we can have a detailed discussion on your requirements.'

'Please do not hesitate to reach out to me for any doubts or clarifications.'

I hit send. A thrill ran through my body.

Of course I would get the sale. I just wanted to do it on my terms.

I got up from my chair to go to the washroom. Not a minute had passed, when I heard the distinct ping of a new email hitting my inbox.

It was Kiran George.

'Hi Surya, thank you for your wonderful email. I appreciate your interest in educating me about the course material. For now, you need not burden yourself with the responsibility of walking me through the course features. I am well aware of Aspire's offerings.'

'If you can share me the payment link at the aforementioned price, I can proceed with the enrolment for the May 1st batch as mentioned in my previous mail.'

'With regards – Kiran George.'

I wasn't one to give up easily.

I shot off another email, this time more passive aggressive.

'Hi Kiran, thank you for your email. It's great to know that you are well aware of Aspire's course features and unique services. However, in order to proceed with the payment, it is imperative that I brief you about the course and the support you will be provided.'

I thought for a while, before adding the following:

'As per company policy.'

There, I put the blame on the company. Now, I would see what Kiran has to say.

I hit send. I went to the kitchen to drink some water.

My inbox pinged again. Kiran George, it was.

'Dude.'

'This is a good deal for you. Take it. Don't deny yourself your incentive by acting over-smart with customers.'

I blew my top. Who the hell was this guy, giving *gyaan* on how to do my job?

Ideally, I should have sent him the payment link and completed the enrolment. But my ego was now in the way.

I shot back an angry email.

'Kiran, thank you for your reply. I am sorry to inform you that we are not offering any discounts on your course of interest. Hence, the course price is Rs.21,234, inclusive of GST.'

'Let me know if you would like to proceed with the EMI options for credit card, as provided by our payment gateway partner.'

I hit send, again.

There was no response for an hour or so.

I was having lunch with my family, when my phone buzzed loudly.

It was Vijay. Wasn't he on leave?

I ignored the call. He was on a trip to Goa with his college friends. Maybe he was calling to ask if I wanted any souvenir from one of the shacks.

It wasn't until 30 minutes later when I returned back his call.

'Hey Vijay, how are you? How's Goa? Listen, I don't want any souvenirs from there. Don't bother yourself with such things...' he cut me off.

'Shut up. Just, SHUT UP!'

'Vijay, what happened? Do you need some money? Are you at the police station?' my voice was filled with concern.

'You...you punk. I am trying to enjoy a well-deserved holiday with my friends, after sleepless days and nights monitoring and saving you buffoons from Abhishek. The day I am on leave, what does Abhishek call and tell me?'

Crap. So, the news was out. The gossip vine in Aspire was very strong.

'Kiran George, one of our regular customers – has marked the entire sales team of Aspire, along with Ajith, Abhishek and Chavan – the bloody co-founder of the company; stating that one of your sales-person is insulting him on mail by refusing to sell him a course until he comes on call.'

'Vijay, look – I...'

'Abhishek calls me, today morning. Already, I was nursing a bad headache from the party last night. Now, he tells me that I am not a good Team Lead, since I have no clue on how to handle erratic team members and their idiosyncrasies. Abhishek thinks, I am not fit to be a Team Lead anymore.'

'Hope the party was worth it,' I bit my tongue, regretting it immediately.

'Was it worth it? Heck, yes. Now, let me make this month worth your while.'

'I can see that you are on dot with your LTD target. Now, I am going to double your target for the month. If you don't do the new target, I will drop you straight into the PIP.'

I became defensive immediately. 'Vijay, you can't do that. I won't...'

'You won't WHAT? If you have a problem with my methods, resign immediately. Thank your lucky stars, Ajith wanted to kick you out of the company right away for insulting a long-time customer, I calmed him down and said I would talk to you.'

My head started aching. Where was the damn Crocin when you needed it?

'Now, back to business. I am going to another party, Before that, you are going to clean up this mess with Kiran George.'

'Oh yeah? How do I do that?' I asked, acidly.

'Reply back to him, saying – Hi Kiran, apologies for the earlier mail. I did not mean to offend your sensibilities in any manner.'

'In order to extend my sincerest apologies for causing you mental distress, I would like to extend to you the 'Generative AI Essentials' course at the discounted price of Rs.15,000, all inclusive of GST.'

'I am sure this price is agreeable to you. Do let me know when you would like to proceed with the payment, I will share across the link at your earliest convenience.'

'Vijay, I can't do this. What about my honour, my pride, my respect...' I protested.

'Take all of that, and shove it where it belongs. Do as I say, or forget you ever worked at this company.'

With gritted teeth, I typed out the mail word-to-word, as Vijay had stated. I copied Ajith, Abhishek, and Chavan as well, to be on the safe side.

Within 30 seconds, I received a reply.

'Hi Surya, thanks for the mail. I am good to proceed at the new price. Please send me the payment link.'

I shared the payment link across. It was completed instantly.

'Surya, you know something? This Kiran guy, has always paid a minimum of Rs.16,500 for all the courses he has purchased from us. Now, your genius tactic has forced us to lower the price. Next time he comes back, we can never sell him above the price of 15k. See what you've done.'

I was not in a mood for a lecture. 'Yeah, fine. The entire team was going on zero today, anyway. At least, I made a single sale.'

'I think you mean; Prem made the sale.'

My ears perked up. 'I'm sorry, what?'

'It is Prem's pot.'

I checked the CRM dashboard. Sure enough, the owner of the pot was now Prem.

'Vijay, I am very sure that the pot was in my name. When did it become Prem's?'

Vijay grunted. 'I changed it. Did you really think, after all this drama – you would get the sale?'

'Consider this as your punishment. No sale today plus, double your monthly target.'

'Enjoy your day, Surya. I have to get back to my party. Bye!' Vijay hung up.

CHAPTER FOURTEEN

ALL THAT GLITTERS IS ALWAYS GOLD

Anytime there is no sale forthcoming from the lead pipeline, we salespersons resorted to ESR calls.

ESR calls are essentially those incoming calls where customers call up the number flashing on the website; to clarify any doubts or queries they might have about a particular course.

Who takes these calls? No prizes for the answer. We do.

I have never really understood what the full form for ESR stood for – nor have I attempted to find out. All I heard about it was – 'Patience is the key; you just have to keep your eyes peeled and ears open for the right *bakra*...err customer.'

'Surya, anything in the pipeline today?' Raman pinged me.

'No, Raman bhai. Nothing as of now. You have something?'

'Nope, I'm done for the day. Abhishek is in a rage. The whole team is sitting on zero.'

'When is that guy not angry? Even If I score 100/100 in a paper, he will say – 'Why don't you try for 150% of your target? Achieving more never hurt anybody.' Absolute nut, that guy is.'

'Yeah. Listen, keep your ESR on. Calls are getting missed. The leadership is monitoring agents who don't have their ESR on.' Raman messaged.

'Raman bhai, I want to focus on sales now. The only calls I get on ESR are – 'Unable to login,' 'How to change my password,' 'When am I going to get my course completion certificate'...it honestly feels like we are doing Support's job. Where are these guys anyway when the customer needs them?'

'Leave it, Surya. We have only two more hours to go before logoff. Get at least one sale before that. Don't go on zero,' Raman pinged, and went offline.

Reluctantly, I switched on my ESR function in the CRM.

My phone started to ring. Not a moment too soon.

'Thank you reaching Aspire. My name is Surya, how can I assist you today?' I said in a practiced voice.

'Hello?' an arrogant voice thundered on the other side of the call.

'Yes Sir, thank you reaching Aspire. How can I assist you today?'

'Hi, I have still not received my Masala Dosa order. Where is the Diggy delivery boy?'

I felt like smashing my phone onto the wall. I realized that would be futile – the wall would suffer a crack; we just re-painted the house.

'Hello Sir. Thank you for your call. Could you please share the details?' I said.

'Hi, yeah. It's 459037, we had ordered from Swagat Veg Restaurant. Has the order been prepared?'

I decided to have a little fun. I would ask Prem to archive the recording later for memory's sake.

'Hi Sir, yes – we have received your order. Two Chicken Masala Dosas, with special egg gravy and onion chutney.'

I let the moment sink in.

'What? What did you say?'

'Yes Sir. Your order has already been dispatched. The delivery boy is on the way.'

'What nonsense! I say, we are pure Brahmin people. There is some mistake, you have taken the wrong person's order.'

'Oh, is it Sir? May I have your good name, please?'

'Madhavan Iyer,' the customer sounded very agitated.

'I see...let me check my database,' I feigned importance, attempting to ensure I tapped my keyboard keys loud enough for the customer to hear.

'Right, Sir. The issue has been resolved.' I said.

'Has it, really? Thank God.'

'Yes, it has. I am not from Diggy, neither do I have information about your dosa.'

'I'm sorry? Who the hell are you then?'

'I am from Aspire Solutions; we sell online courses to professionals who are looking to upskill themselves in the competitive Information and Technology space.'

Madhavan could not believe what he was hearing. 'You're not from Diggy?'

'No, Sir.'

'Then why the hell did you waste my time?' he screamed.

'Thank you reaching Aspire. Have a great day. I hope your dosas reach you on time.' I chuckled.

'You scoundrel...I will have you hanged...bloody rascal!'

'Please let us know how we can improve our services. Feel free to rate our call on a scale of 1 to 5, 1 standing for 'Not satisfactory' to 5 standing for 'Very satisfied,' I continued in a monotone.

'You don't have anything on a negative scale?' Madhavan growled. I am not sure if that was his voice or his tummy.

'We hope we were able to resolve your query. Have a great day ahead!' I hung up the call, and switched off my ESR to block incoming calls.

I tried wasting some more time before my official log-off time at 11 PM. I saw Abhishek's ping again, in our team group.

'Why is the entire Group sitting on zero today? Are you all not ashamed of yourselves?'

Tired and frustrated? Maybe, a little.

Ashamed? In your dreams.

I saw Vijay replying. 'We are trying our level best to make sure we get connects with pots. I am personally monitoring to see if all the agents have their ESR on or not.'

Oops, I switched on my ESR back again.

A notification popped up in my WhatsApp window. It was Vijay.

'You are not logging off today without getting a sale. Beg, borrow, steal – do whatever. Todays' team score will be updated by you only in the group.'

'Why don't you ask me to shave my head and dance naked in public instead? I can't face Abhishek.'

'Dancing naked in public is easier than a meeting with Abhishek. I will also join you, if necessary.'

That motivated me. 'Yes, boss. I will find something before logoff.' I closed the chat window.

My phone started to vibrate. It was an ESR call. 'Is it another Diggy fellow, Godammit,' I whined.

Before picking the call, I checked the number on my CRM database. It was an old prospect, who had done activity on the Docker course six months ago.

'Email id is _sahniforyou799@gmail.com_. Hmm, the pot is under Vaishnav, Closed Lost; 7 months ago.'

'Reason for Closed Lost – Arrogant customer, thinks he knows more than Bill Gates.'

Vaishnav was a team member from the other Group, which typically handled Cloud courses – a cash cow for the Aspire sales team.

If this guy was calling, there really must be something.

'Thank you reaching Aspire, my name is Surya – how can I assist you today?'

'Hey Surya, how are you doing? Jaideep this side,' a polished voice spoke on the other line.

'Hi Jaideep, I'm doing good; how are you? Let me know how I can assist you.'

'Yes, I need assistance. Why is the payment gateway on your website not working?'

My ears perked up; my fingers tingled. I knew that feeling.

This guy was a payment.

'Hi Jaideep, what seems to be the issue?'

'Well, I am trying to pay for the May 6th batch of the live Docker course, but the payment gateway does not seem to have credit card EMI options. Is there a glitch, or is there something you guys know that I am yet to find out about?'

'Jaideep, not an issue. The thing is, EMI options via the website page has not been enabled.'

'Oh damn, that's bad. I don't have the cash to pay the full amount right away. Let me see next month after I clear my credit card dues,' Jaideep resigned to his fate.

'But,' I paused for a second.

'But...what?' Jaideep replied.

'I can send you a payment link from my end, which has EMI options enabled. Additionally, I will give you a Rs.2000 flat discount on the course fee for the inconvenience caused.'

I bit my tongue. Never give a discount to a customer, unless they ask for it.

Vijay would bury me alive. We would take care of that later.

'Oh, wow! I didn't know such a provision was available. Yes, please send me the payment link for 3 months EMI.'

'Sure Sir. Preferred bank?'

'IDIDI.'

'Okay, enabling the link now,' my fingers splattered over the keyboard.

Then, it hit me.

The pot was not in my name. If the sale came through, the system would recognize that Vaishnav has sent the payment link and immediately add the sale onto his name.

I decided to rally my weapons arsenal.

SOO: Switch of Ownership.

The concept of SOO was simple. In the event that a sales agent from the same or different team chances upon a paying prospect who has been marked as 'Closed Lost' a long time ago, and the concerned agent who had to follow-up with the prospect has not done so, or has resigned to her/his fate that the pot is not a paying one – a SOO can be dropped.

Of course, it is not as simple as it sounds. It is something of a Constitution document created by one of the founding members of the company, to avoid fights or confusion among agents regarding conflicting payments.

Fights happened anyway. How did having a guiding book make any difference?

I pinged Vijay. 'Vijay, listen. I have a paying pot on the line. Pot is in Vaishnav's name. I'm dropping the SOO. Please change it to my name.'

He replied instantly. 'Good. I am ready. Drop the SOO.'

'Hey, are you sending the payment link? I am waiting on the line,' Jaideep said, a hint of irritation in his voice.'

'Hey Jaideep, sorry for the delay. The payment link is getting verified for security purposes from the gateway's side. I am reconciling with IDIDI to ensure that the EMI options are available on the link.'

'Oh ok, I didn't know there were so many technicalities to carry out. No issues, I'll wait.'

I type out the SOO mail, and dropped it Vaishnav, marking a copy to Vijay.

Preparing the payment link took me less than 30 seconds. I sent it out as well.

'Hey, I got the link. Do I pay now?' Jaideep asked.

'Hi, yes Jaideep. The EMI options have already been selected. You can proceed with the payment right away.'

I got a ping. It was Vaishnav.

'You think you can pull a fast one on me? I am going to talk to Vijay about this,' he pinged.

'Go ahead, dude. This baby is mine today.'

I checked the payment status. Jaideep had completed the payment. Almost immediately, Vijay had switched the pot to my name.

'Hi, Surya. Payment done. I have received the login details as well. So, anything else I have to do?'

'Nothing else, Jaideep. Any questions on the course, please feel free to reach out to Vaishnav. He will be the support person assigned to you on this engagement.'

'Oh? Isn't it going to be you? Since you are the guy who helped me complete the payment.'

'Absolutely. I will be going on a month-long leave, starting from today. In the event you are unable to reach me via email or text, Vaishnav will be more than happy to help you with your queries.'

'Surya, update the score in the team group,' Vijay pinged.

Abhishek was happy that we did not go on zero. Instead, I had brought in 18k worth of revenue to the company on a dry day.

'Why did you give Jaideep a discount when he didn't ask for it?' Vijay pinged, adding an angry emoji.

I ignored his message, and went offline. Done for the day.

It was true that Vaishnav did the baking – but the cake would be mine to eat!

CHAPTER FIFTEEN

WHY SALES?

Shouldn't this story be in the beginning of the book? As in, the 'why' is always answered first, isn't it?

Point taken. Consider this story as a mid-book crisis, or a mid-job crisis. After close to eight months into the job, an internal panic started to develop inside me, that I might be in the wrong profession and selling just wasn't for me.

After much thought, I decided to talk to one of my mentors in the company – Sandeep Nair. We used to affectionately call him Sandeep *Chetta*. Chetta stood for 'Big Brother' in Malayalam.

'Hi Chetta, how are you?'

'Hey Surya. Good to hear from you after such a long time. You have forgotten about me, isn't it?'

'*Aiyo*, nothing like Chetta. I was just busy with work, targets...you know how it is.'

Sandeep Chetta had joined Aspire when he was an intern. Due to his top performance, solid selling skills and closing techniques, he was today heading a team of 10 salespeople.

'Cut the bullshit, I'm not your customer. Now, tell me why you wanted to have this conversation.'

I adjusted my mike. 'Chetta, to be honest – I'm feeling very stagnated in my current job. I don't think I am cut out for this.'

'Why Surya, what's wrong? I see you doing your targets regularly. Any issues with a difficult customer?'

'No Chetta, it's not that. I'm just finding the work very repetitive. We live on targets and our lives are determined on how the end of the month turns out.'

'Exactly when we feel that a bad month has gone by, the next month's target has begun, a rollercoaster of sorts commences once again.'

Sandeep Chetta did not reply for a few seconds.

'Ok, I hear you. What do you need from me?'

'I want to understand why you have stuck around in sales for so long. I mean, it has been close to 6 years for you in this company, right? After a point – didn't you feel that this job wasn't what you wanted?'

Sandeep Chetta did not believe in long answers. Any advice or sales pitch, had to be to the point.

'You can take an individual out of sales, never sales out of an individual.'

I was dumbfounded. 'I'm sorry, what?'

Sandeep Chetta ignored my comment. He continued in a monotone.

'I'm not somehow who motivates people. What you need, is a little push and incentive to get back into the race. Do you know the biggest motivator for any salesperson?'

I shot a guess. 'I don't know...promotions, maybe?'

'You should be a comedian. No, that's not the answer.'

'The biggest motivator for a salesperson, is money. Simple, plain – money,' Sandeep Chetta said.

'Didn't the VP of sales tell us money isn't everything, customer satisfaction is?' I asked.

'Which is why he is the VP and you are still a lowly agent. Look, If I want a promotion – I will get it anyway, if my sales are good. If I want a better designation, the company can create a role and give it to me, or fire the guy who isn't doing his job, then I replace him.'

'So, the incentive you get upon achieving your target – is the biggest motivator.'

A few gears started to rotate in my mind. 'Go on, this is a new perspective.'

'Sales makes or breaks people, there is no question about it. People hate sales for the fact that it is a 24x7 job with practically no holidays. Taking a week off could potentially get you fired or replaced, as the company can find someone else to do your job better than you – the job is so volatile in nature. There is anxiety and tension even on holidays.'

'For example, I freak out when I don't have access to my office mail. I need to know what's going on. If I am on a holiday, I know for a fact I could have created 2 lakhs worth of revenue instead of sitting on a beach sipping orange juice. The pressure is real, and the churn is faster in sales, than any other business function.'

'Really? Why is that?'

'We bring in the money for the company, don't we? Kind of like, the bread-winners.'

'Only the best survive. Right now, what you are experiencing is normal. There are ups and downs in every job. Sales, on the other hand, works like the stock market. The highs are very high, it can be overwhelming at times. But the lows, well – there are very bad lows, somewhere beneath the lowest tunnel you can find.'

'Yes, exactly my point. The lows are pathetic. Why stay in sales, then?'

'Because of the money. Let me explain. Last month, I achieved 110% of my target. I bought a bike and a brand-new phone only through my incentive,' Sandeep Chetta grinned.

My mouth dropped wide open. 'What the...you're not serious.'

'Of course, I am. There are glory days in sales too. Some months are too good. I got sent to Malaysia by the company as an incentive for achieving my target for the full fiscal year. Uff, an all-expenses paid trip. That was a good time, 'Sandeep Chetta sighed.

I rubbed my chin in deep thought. 'So, you're saying, focus on the money.'

'Yes, exactly. If you are here right now, it means you have some selling abilities within you. Not everyone has that. Its God given, learn to appreciate it, Surya.'

'What if I say money does not motivate me?' I questioned.

'Then you are an idiot. Why not work for free then?' Chetta said.

'The biggest adrenaline rush for me is when I see that incentive hit my bank account and rubbing that inflated bank balance in front of my friends who earn a fixed salary month on month, irrespective of performance.'

'Hey, but that's...' I tried to interrupt.

'Yes, I know what you are about to say. Understand, this is just me speaking. What I'm espousing, will not apply for everyone. This has worked for me; I am not saying it will work for you.'

I was not convinced.

'Yes, I understand. But, are we even making a difference to people's lives? I mean, we are just looking out for ourselves here.'

'I don't understand. Do you want open an NGO? We do make a difference to people's lives. I have so many messages from my customers who have completed their courses and bagged a promotion within a year. What better impact can you think of? Goodwill and money, are my biggest motivators.'

'You know, someone told me that a credit card salesperson, earns more in incentives than the guy he is selling the card to,' I said.

'There you go. You seem to have all the answers. Why did you want this call, again?'

'I wanted you to sell 'sales' to me. I think you did a pretty good job.' I said, with a cheeky smile.

'Funny guy. Bye, Surya. I hope I convinced you to stay. If not, all the best for your charity work.'

CHAPTER SIXTEEN

CUSTOMER GYAAN

'Here's the thing, folks. Follow-ups are what makes the sale worth it.'

I was snoring loudly, with my mike on.

'Follow-ups, Mr. Surya – are what makes a SALE WORTH IT? Do you understand?'

Hearing my name being called out of the blue, I woke up instantly. Without further ado, I adjusted my headset and first muted myself.

'You there, Mr. Surya? Or am I straining your attention to the extent that you have fallen asleep in my session, once again?'

Trivedi's training sessions for Aspire's agents were a pain. It was more theory and less practical. Imagine, learning how to swim by reading a textbook.

That, in one short line – was Trivedi style.

Having composed myself, I unmuted my mike.

'Yes, Sir. I am here, all good and ready. Actually, my mixie's motor is having some issues, you might have thought I was snoring,' I said.

'We didn't think, everyone in this meeting was pretty sure...,' I cut him off.

'Absolutely not, Trivedi Sir. Why would I sleep in a session as interesting as yours? I know for a fact you were talking about how paramount follow-ups are for salespeople. I hope I got that right?'

'Hmm, yes. In fact, that is what I was talking about. Good, at least it shows you were listening. Get that mixie fixed quickly,' Trivedi said.

'Yes Sir, absolutely,' I said. I muted my mike once again, falling back on the couch to continue my nap.

'Alright. So, coming to follow-ups. Why is it so important? Anyone in the meeting can answer?'

Alisha raised a virtual hand.

'Yes, Alisha. Go ahead.'

'Follow-ups ensure that we are in constant contact with a customer for a sale. It once happened to me, that the customer said he would pay tomorrow, but did not return my calls or text for a week.'

'I see. Then, what did you do?'

'I constantly followed up with him to ensure that I was in his sights. A few weeks of follow-up later, the customer revealed that a close relative in his family had passed away, and he was not in the state of mind to pursue any course in his current mental make-up.'

'He was happy that I reminded him about his intent to pursue the course. Post which, he paid immediately.'

'Fantastic. Thank you, Alisha. That was a wonderful example. Anyone else would like to add to the discussion?'

There was no answer. Only their smiling virtual pictures were visible, with everyone's mikes muted.

Trivedi growled. 'Well, it seems like everyone here is an expert salesperson. Fine.'

He glanced at his watch. 'I have 5 more minutes to go, before I end this session. Since you duffers already know so much about sales and lead pursuits, let me enlighten you all with a small analogy.'

'Try and imagine this beautiful girl walking on the street. She is in a hot chili red dress, red lipstick, and a yellow colour handbag.'

Multiple cameras were instantly switched on. Chari, one of the agents, unmuted and spoke.

'Trivedi Sir, we are imagining. Continue, please.'

'Quiet. Now, all the boys in the neighbourhood are behind her. She has a nice walk and a pleasing personality, with a laugh as sweet as nectar.'

'Okay, then?' I was awake now.

'Quiet, let me finish.'

'She shops only at the branded stores. Her parents are rich, they own half the city. She has the resources to get anyone she wants; go anywhere she wants – date any one she desires.'

'But there is one catch to this entire story,' Trivedi said.

'She is not the typical rich girl, you know – spoilt brat types. She always sees the good in people. So, one day, she happens to meet this handsome, poor, underpaid industrial worker who seemingly has a heart of gold.'

'How the heck do you know he was underpaid?' Shoumin, a senior agent asked.

'He was based on you. Any other stupid questions?' The entire call become silent again.

'Continuing the story: the girl and boy meet under unexpected circumstances. She sees him helping an old couple cross the road at the supermarket junction. The goodness in her sees him as her future partner. Their eyes meet, their hearts flutter. A meeting of two souls, designed to be together forever.'

I wasn't able to understand head or tail on what Trivedi was getting at. Nevertheless, I was curious on how the story would end.

'The girl and boy meet, they exchange numbers. The girl proposes that they meet up later in the day. The boy agrees, saying that he would meet her near the massive city bridge at dusk.'

'As dusk approached, the girl sat on the sole bench near the city bridge. She waited for her true love. An hour passed.'

'Another hour went by, but the boy never showed up.'

'The girl was visibly disappointed. She goes to bed, crying all night.'

'The next day, the girl arrives at the same junction for some shopping. Eyes puffy from crying last night, she glances across the road.'

'And what does she see? The same boy – her one and true love – helping the same old couple cross the road. But this time, there was someone else looking at the boy.'

'It was her neighbour from her fancy neighbourhood. It looked like the neighbour had fallen for the boy's goodness as well.'

'As the boy was about to exchange numbers with the neighbour, the rich girl flew into a fit of rage. She ran across the junction and confronted the boy. She told her neighbour the entire story, and forced a confession out of the boy.'

'It seemed that the old couple was in the pay of the boy as well. He had been unable to turn up the previous night since he was busy trying to extract money from another innocent woman.'

'That's the end of the story. Any questions?' Trivedi asked.

I raised a virtual hand in the meeting.

'Yes, Surya. You have a question?'

'Yeah, quite a big one, actually. Do you mind telling me the point of narrating this story?'

'Oh sure. Didn't you guess it already?'

'Uhh, no. I believe the audience is clueless.'

'It's pretty simple. Always give more importance to an existing customer.'

'So, you're saying – the girl in the red dress was the existing customer?'

'Yes. If the boy had turned up the other night, instead of trying to acquire a new target to scam, he might have just found true love – and true money.'

'Then, you are implying that we agents scam customers? And we are poor and underpaid?'

'Did I say anything wrong?' Trivedi asked.

'No, you were absolutely spot on. I just don't understand why you had to make up such a cock and bull story to make a simple point.'

'You've heard of *Panchatantra*? Maybe, *Vikram-Vedha* tales?'

'Yes, what about them?'

'The whole point of the story was – it is much more effective to retain an existing customer, rather than trying to poach a new one, which is a much more expensive proposition.'

I was not impressed. 'I wonder how long it took you to come up with this story,' I mused, loudly.

'Long enough to justify my hourly fees,' Trivedi grunted and logged out of the call.

I heard my phone buzz. It was an existing customer, probably calling me for a support issue.

I cut the call. I focused on the new leads which were getting added to my pipeline.

'I just hope the guys implement what Trivedi was saying. He described the girl very well.'

THIS MEETING COULD HAVE BEEN AN EMAIL

'Check your mail, dude. Ajith has setup a meeting.'

Prem had pinged me on WhatsApp. It was 9 AM in the morning. I was sprawling in my bed, half awake and drooling on my pillow.

Irritated, I picked up my phone and checked the notification.

'What's his problem?' I wrote back.

'Don't know, dude. Something about Year End targets.'

Great. Another meeting to discuss what we would be doing in upcoming meetings.

I never liked meetings. They were created by people who loved to talk endlessly about a goal which neither the company nor its people would ever achieve, and demand the attention span of people who would rather watch a movie than listen to their boss's monotone.

On top of that – meeting notes.

'Can someone please take the notes of the meeting?'

'Please make sure the meeting notes adhere to the format used last time.'

'Ensure that the notes capture everything, both positive and negative points. Don't leave anything out, be as transparent as possible.'

The first time I was taking meeting notes, I wrote the points in all sincerity.

A few folks had logged off from the online meeting in the middle. I noted down their names and jotted it under the meeting notes, emailing the list to the entire team.

A senior manager made me understand that this was not a school and I was not a class monitor, gently threatening me to stick to my job scope or else I would have to find another one. I have repeated the same error multiple times – the senior manager is now in another job.

I doubt if anyone ever read the meeting notes from the last meeting. What was the point? By the time we approached the next meeting in the upcoming week, our objective would have completely changed. It was like deciding to go to Chandigarh by flight in our last meeting, but now are now on the way to Italy by foot.

'Prem bro, what time is the meeting?'

'It's at 11 PM, tonight.'

11 PM was my logout time. I silently cursed Ajith, secretly hoping that he got locked out of his house or suffered some kind of indigestion. I hated working beyond my stipulated working hours, unless it was the week before Month End.

'Forget it, I'm out.' I messaged back.

'Dude, everyone must attend. You missed the last meeting as well.'

I gave up. Not attending two meetings in a row was seen as a compliance issue.

'Yeah fine, 11 PM is it? I'll login on time.' I threw my phone across the bed.

As 11 PM drew closer, the team WhatsApp Group came alive.

'Guys, Ajith is calling. Login asap, now,' Vijay messaged in our team group.

'Sure, Vijay – joining,' I pinged.

I joined the 11 PM call. The entire big brass of the company was there. There were easily 150 or more people in the call. Some folks had their video on, their faces sleep deprived, with dark circles under their eyes.

I noticed someone switch on their video. It was the Man of the Moment – Ajith.

'Hi team, how are we doing today?' Ajith spoke, in his polished voice.

'Doing good, Ajith,' Sharon, one of the team leads, replied.

'Can someone take the notes of the meeting? Vijay, any recommendations?'

'Surya will do it. Surya, you will take the notes, right?'

'Sure, Vijay.'

'Great. We are good to go. Let's get started then.'

I listened in, intently.

'So, guys, we are now approaching December 31st, which is the Calendar Year End. I want you guys to push yourself and give your best. The company has some stipulated targets to achieve, which has already been circulated to your Team Leads.'

'All the best. That's it from my side.'

Ajith switched off his video, and logged out of the meeting.

I sat on my chair, dumbfounded. That's it? What the heck was I supposed to write in the meeting notes?

I could see many disgruntled faces in the meeting. One guy was visibly angry and was hurling abuses with his camera on; but mike switched off. Another girl was talking loudly in a language I did not understand, with her video switched off. No one seemed happy.

How could I ensure that the management never pulled a stunt like this on us again?

Then, it hit me.

I punched out the summary of Ajith's sermon, with the subject line –

'This meeting could have been an email.'

I almost hit send, when I realized that my phone EMI was bigger than my ego.

CHAPTER EIGHTEEN

FOLLOW-UP: TO FOLLOW THROUGH

'Any sales, *macha*?' Venky asked me.

'No Venky, nothing as of now. I am tired of this job. None of the pots are picking my call.'

Venky was my good friend from another Group. We initially met when both our team leads were fighting over a payment.

Both of us were the guys initiating the fight and then backing off when things become heated, to watch the fun unfold between our leads. I would say we connected well on fights.

'It's ok, *macha*. Just be patient. Indian customers are like that.'

Venky had more than 3 years of experience, that was 2 and a half years more than me in this job. If he was saying something, it had to make sense.

'See *macha*, you have to treat the customer like you are going for a date.'

'A date?' I was confused.

'Yes. Assume that you are going on a date with this really pretty girl.'

I already started imagining. 'Absolutely. I am already assuming.'

'Okay, great. Now, you don't know each other from before. Both of you are courting each other, checking out social media profiles, work experience, likes-dislikes etc.'

'Venky, what does this have to do with sales?'

'Wait *macha*, always in a hurry for everything! Now, you decide to meet up on the first date. Imagine, this is like making the first call to the customer.'

'Now things make sense. Go on.'

'On the first date, both of you are very nice to each other. You want to make a good impression, you flatter each other, pay some compliments, wine, and dine etc.'

'Which means to say – we salespeople are all nice to a customer on the first call? And the customer, nice to us?' I asked.

'Absolutely, you got it. Now, the date is coming to a close. You decide to pay the bill, since you would like a second date. But the girl is smart.'

'She knows for a fact that there are multiple smart, handsome, and charming boys giving her attention. Why would she stick with you, when she has multiple options to choose from?'

'And, the multiple boys would be...other competitor salespeople?'

'You are catching on. Back to the story. You call this girl for a second date, you WhatsApp here, you SMS her. No response. Sound familiar?'

'Yes, very. Too good to be true.'

'Why would she? This is the phase where you need to show your patience. And your follow-ups.'

'Venky, if she wanted a second date – she would call, right? What nonsense, why would I go behind her?'

'That's where you are wrong. First assess the situation. Do you think she is the only guy you are talking to?'

I felt my brain rewire itself. Venky's analogy and my relationship status in real life were getting intertwined with each other.

'What do you do? You follow-up. Send some nice poetry, every once in two days. Maybe, surprise her with a nice gift on her birthday. Not to the extent when it gets too creepy and she reports you to the police.'

'So, you're saying – follow-up regularly, keep sending the customer reminders that you exist and ensure you're in the customer's good books?'

'Playing the hard game always, does not work. Show your softer side, show that you care for her.'

'You want me to become a softie?'

'The point is to ensure that you are constantly in the customer's radar. Out of sight, is out of mind.'

'Fantastic. So, do I get the girl or not?' I asked, impatiently.

'That really depends on how persistent you are. Either that, or you must have the charm of SRK or the looks of Hrithik. In your case, I would say being persistent would work for you.'

'Don't you have confidence in my charm or looks?' I mewed.

'No one in their right mind should.' Venky guffawed.

'Ay, Venky, what *da.*'

'I have a call right now. See you later, all the best,' Venky logged out of the meeting.

Venky was someone I respected deeply. Why not try out his technique? I decided to do it immediately.

One of the customer accounts I was handling was being very unresponsive. In our initial call, the customer was extremely sweet and was talking very well, promising me a group deal once he had spoken to his company HR person.

Post that call, I had not heard from him for the past 2 weeks. I thought – 'Maybe he is busy, why should I disturb him? If he wants the course, he will surely come back to me.'

All of a sudden, Venky's analogy dawned upon me.

It wasn't a bad date. The girl clearly liked me, but she wanted to know if I was in for the long haul. How serious was I about this relationship?

I opened the call list of my phone and dialled the customer number. I had named his contact as – 'Chandok Group Deal'

Not surprisingly, he did not pick up. I tried again.

This time, he cut my call.

Unfazed, I dropped him a follow-up mail.

'Hey Chandok, hope you are doing well.'

'As per our last conversation, you had shown interest in the 'AI for Managers' course at Aspire Solutions. Do let me know if you or your colleagues need any additional details from my end, to proceed with the enrolment.'

'Thanks, and regards – Surya.'

I put a follow-up date of 3 days from the date of the mail.

Three days passed by. I was determined to implement this policy for all my pots.

I dialled Chandok's number again. Again, he did not pick up.

WhatsApp, it is.

Venky had mentioned something else – always playing hardball with the customer does not work. Maybe, if I tried a new technique?

I typed the following message.

'Hey Chandok, hope all is well.'

'I understand that you may not be keeping well, or maybe busy at the workplace due to a sudden change in schedule.'

'I would like to take this opportunity to let you know, that I will be keeping the offer on hold for as long as it takes. When you are ready, ping me and we can take the deal forward at your convenience.'

The colourless double tick sign flashed. Thank God, at least he had not blocked me.

A minute later, I noticed the double ticks turn blue. So, he had read my message. That was a good start.

Chandok started typing feverishly.

'Hey Surya, thank you for your message. My team is currently undergoing a change, due to some performance issues and team members resigning. I am unsure of when the transition will be complete.'

'Until then, please keep the offer open for me. I confirm that four of my colleagues will enrol with me as discussed in our first call.'

'Thanks, once again.'

I was happy. I forwarded this text to Venky.

He called me immediately. 'Surya, ask him for a follow-up date now.' Venky said.

'What? Why, is it necessary? He said he will come back to me.'

'Yes, that is what they all say. Now, you provide him the follow-up date. Say, one week from now.'

'Venky, he is undergoing a crisis at his office. I need to be more understanding.'

'Are you dating this guy? Shut up and listen to me. Tell him, you will keep this offer on hold – but only for the next two weeks, that is until month end.'

'If he is unwilling to enrol until then, ask him to take a walk.'

'Venky, what about being a softie?'

'Yes, that phase is over. Now, time to mean business. *Chalo*, I will catch you later. Bye.' Venky hung up.

I was confused. It seemed like Venky was giving me contradictory advice. I wanted to be nice, but Venky has asked me to give the customer a hard deadline.

I threw my conscience into the dustbin. 'Let me listen to Venky, this time round. Next time, do it your way.'

I saw my WhatsApp ping. It was Venky. 'Send this text to the customer. Tell me how he responds.'

I opened his message.

'Hi Chandok, thanks for the update. I just had a word with my Team Lead regarding your situation.'

'Unfortunately, he is very strict about the deadline we generally keep an offer on hold for. I tried reasoning with him, but he has refused to accommodate your case.'

'He has allowed me to keep the offer open only until next week, post which the deal will be rescinded. I hope you understand my situation. Looking forward to your views in this matter.'

I didn't like it. I typed back.

'Venky, not happening bro. This is very impersonal.'

'Do as I say,' Venky pinged back, and went offline.

I took a deep breath. Here's to another month of not doing target. I long held the message, and forwarded it to Chandok.

The blue ticks came on instantly. There was no response for the next hour.

I lost hope altogether. 'I am done.' I proceeded to Instagram to unfriend Venky.

My phone pinged. Chandok had replied back.

'Hey Surya, I did not expect this message from you, especially in a time when I am handling an urgent matter at office. Right now, I cannot give any definite response.'

'Let's connect next week, I will think of whether I want to move ahead with you guys or not.'

I hit a thumbs up on his message and shut my laptop, howling loudly, and wishing Venky fell into a well.

A week later, I followed up with Chandok. This time, he picked up.

'Hey Chandok, hope all is well. I...'

'Surya, thanks so much for calling. Can I pay now?'

'Sorry, what?'

'Can we get the enrolment done right away? I have the HR's approval to move ahead. Let's do this fast? I have a meeting in a few minutes.'

'Yes...YES! Of course we can go ahead. But tell me, is your office issue resolved?' I asked.

'No, not in totality. To be honest, I was in talks with a few other institutes along with Aspire as well. What I liked about you guys; was you were not trying to force the course down my throat like the others. That was real empathy that you guys showed.'

'Since I had a deadline of a week's time, I went behind my HR, in charge of Learning and Development to get the approval done. Well, here I am.'

I was a little flustered. 'But, didn't you feel bad that Venky...I mean my Team Lead said you just had a week to figure out if you wanted to take the course or not.'

'Yes, I understand that. It was a business decision and no hard feelings. You have targets to achieve and so do we,' Chandok said.

'Nice...sure, that was great, Chandok. I will share the group enrolment link with you now. Please check your mail.'

Post logoff, I gave Venky a virtual biryani party by ordering veg cutlets and chicken biryani to his house address.

Follow-up, to follow through!

CHAPTER NINETEEN

PIP: THE BRIDGE BETWEEN HEAVEN AND HELL

The PIP is a dreaded place to be in, even for the most accomplished employee.

Performance Improvement Program, lovingly called as the PIP.

Salespersons who had not achieved their target for three months on a consecutive basis, were dropped into the PIP. Then, they were given a target to accomplish within 1 week.

If they hit their target, they would be out of the PIP with a warning. If not...well, use your imagination.

One of my team-mates – Akash, happened to run himself into trouble by landing into a PIP.

'Dude, what the hell is wrong with you. At this time of the year, you don't even have to make an effort to sell the courses. It's appraisal season – these pots literally run after us to purchase a course,' I said.

'I'm trying, dude. What do you think I have been doing all this time? None of the pots are picking up my calls; as it is my leads are complete shit. Does Abhishek listen? No. Does Ajith listen? Forget it.'

'Did you talk to Vijay?'

'He said his hands are tied. None of the sales heads are ready to listen to him or me. That's it, I'm done in this company.'

I tried to cheer him up. 'Hey listen, let me do one thing. I'll talk to Raman, he'll silently put Athulya's pots in your name. No one will know.'

Akash's voice became wild.

'You will do nothing of this sort. I don't want to cover one blunder by committing another one. I got into the PIP on my own terms, now I will get out of it on my own terms,' he said, sternly.

Akash had high ideals, which was commendable. But even he knew deep inside that the chances of getting out of a PIP was less than 5%. Every day, there would be a call with Vijay and the HR person assessing Akash's sales pipeline, what he had in store for the next day, and whether he was on track to complete his target.

It was a death hole, and there was no way for him to come out of it.

Akash was a fine fellow, too idealistic for my liking and unlike someone who would easily manipulate the customer for his own gains. It was unfortunate that the company was now looking at him as a liability and a number instead of a good human being.

Unless...

The next day, I rang up Akash.

'Hey, how did the meeting with Vijay go?' I asked.

'Yeah, it was fine. Not too bad, Vijay seemed positive that I would do it,' Akash sounded confident.

Vijay was always a good liar.

'Oh, is it? I heard your target was 1 lakh this week?'

'Yes. If I complete it, I am out of the PIP.'

'So, that means around 10 sales of 10k each, right?'

Akash laughed. 'Dude, what are the chances? 10 sales in a week? Never seen that happen before.'

'Let's see. I have a call with a customer, dropping off now. All the best.'

Akash put on his headphone and checked his mail for new leads. The leads were slow, dead slow. In a PIP, the rate of fresh leads to the candidate was limited to near zero – it was an unwritten rule that the candidate had to hunt on old or existing leads to make their target.

His phone started to buzz. It was an unknown number.

Akash picked it up. 'Hello?'

'Is this Akash from Aspire?' the voice on the other line said.

'Yes...I mean, hello Ma'am. Thank you for reaching Aspire, how can I assist you today?'

'Hi, Akash. I am looking to purchase the Big Data course at Aspire. I want the March 4th batch. Is it available?'

Akash checked his computer. 'Yes Ma'am, we have a few slots for the date you had requested for. Can I go ahead and brief you on...' the customer cut him off.

'Akash, I am aware of the course details. Do you mind sharing me the payment link for Rs.16,000?'

Akash felt the wind get knocked out of his chest.

'What the...sorry? You want to pay now? Like, right now?'

'Yes. Did you not hear me, Akash? No negotiations, please. I am not going to pay a single rupee more than 16k. That's my final price.'

Akash could not believe his luck. 'Yes, yes! Of course, I understand. We can lock it in at 16k. Would like to proceed with an EMI option or full payment?'

An hour before logoff, Vijay and the HR person connected with Akash.

'So, Akash, was your day?' Nandita, the HR person asked.

Akash was about to answer, when Vijay interrupted him.

'Why wouldn't it be great? He just made a sale worth 16k.'

'Wow, Akash – that's great news! A good start. If I may ask, how did you get the lead?' Nandita was curious.

Akash though for a while. 'She didn't mention where she got my number. The moment she called, I created a fresh lead in the system and closed her.'

'And, you have no information about her background, designation, company...?' Vijay asked.

'No, nothing of that sort.'

'Well, fine by me. As long as you do your target this week, I'm happy. What say, Nandita?'

'I couldn't agree more, Vijay. Akash, all the very best for the rest of the week. Let me know if you need anything.' Nandita logged out of the meeting.

'Akash, stay back please.' Vijay said.

Vijay came on video.

'Akash, tell me something. This entire day, you made only a single sale. What were you doing for the rest of the day?'

'Vijay, my leads for the day are limited. Look at the number of calls I have taken today, close to 150. My incoming calls are always on, I haven't missed any call today.'

'Yes, I can see that. I'm just wondering how you missed your target for 3 months in a row, got into a PIP; then exactly on the first day of the PIP – you get a sale out of nowhere.'

'Curious case, isn't it?'

Akash bristled at Vijay's comment.

'People go through bad phases Vijay. We're like cricketers, aren't we?'

'Today hero if we hit a century, tomorrow zero if we go on a duck.'

'Akash, that's what sales is about. Anyway, I was just curious. Don't let things like these get on your nerves. I'll see you later, bye.' Vijay dropped off the call.

The next day, something similar happened.

Akash had got a sale from one of his old customers. It wasn't enough, just a small deal for about 5k in revenue. 'How will I manage the rest of the week? I have almost 80k more to go.' Akash thought to himself.

A few minutes later, an unknown number flashed on his phone. He picked it up.

'Hello?'

'Hey Akash, I'm Shubhangi. I want to purchase the Python Fundamentals course from you guys. Any slot available on the weekends?'

'Hello Ma'am, hi. I'm Akash from Aspire, and I'm...'

'Yes, all that is fine. Any slots on the weekends?'

'Ma'am, sorry. Just a second, please? May I know where you got my number from?'

'I'm getting another call. Maybe, let's do the enrolment later?' Shubhangi said.

Akash yelped. How did it matter – whom, what, where and why? He wasn't from the CBI.

'Sure Ma'am, sorry once again. We have a batch coming up this Saturday and Sunday. Would you like to go for that?'

'Yes, that sounds good. And, I can pay only 15k. I hope we can go ahead with this deal.'

Negotiation wasn't a great idea in a place like the PIP. What God gave; one took.

'Perfect, we can lock it in at that price. I'll share the payment link right away. May I have your mail id, please?'

'What, again?' Vijay bellowed.

'Yes, Vijay. What can I say? Luck is on my side.'

'Hey, wipe that grin off. Something is wrong here.'

'Why do you care? I am doing my target, isn't that enough?' Akash shot back.

Vijay was silent. 'Fine. But remember, if you are doing any goofing around with other's pots behind my back, I'll...'

'What? When I do my target, you have a problem. When I don't, you have a problem. Can't you make up your mind?' Akash said with a sudden burst of confidence.

Vijay's face turned red.

'Get out of the PIP, fast,' Vijay muttered and left the meeting.

For the next 3 days, it was the same story over and over again. A caller from an unknown number would promptly ring up Akash around noon and buy a course without any explanation or negotiation.

Vijay stopped asking any questions. He knew something was going on, he just couldn't put a finger on what it was. Obviously, it was not his headache to solve. He liked Akash as a person, but as a Team Lead, he had to play his part.

The faster he was out of the PIP; he would have one more hand to help him achieve his Team's target. In sales, there was nothing like charity – only give and take.

A few days later, Akash called me.

'Hey Akash, what's up?'

'Asshole. You didn't think I would figure out what was happening?'

'I'm sorry?' I said, innocently.

'All the pots who called me and paid without any questions asked – they're your friends, aren't they?'

'I don't think I understand what you mean,' I retorted.

'One of the pots blurted that she had got my number from you. It wasn't hard to connect the dots from there.'

'Hey, listen – I didn't...'

'Look, Surya. All I want to say is, thank you. Thank you for doing this, or else I may not have achieved my target and got out of the PIP. I will say that my favourite part of the entire drama was seeing Abhishek's expression change, when he heard that I had achieved my target.'

'Ha ha, I can understand. You are now part of the 5% club, then.'

'All's well that ends well. I hope we can meet soon in person, Surya. Bye.'

My college friends all had requirements for courses as part of their appraisal process. Obviously, they reached out to me. I simply forwarded Akash's contact to them, explaining the situation to them. The rest is history.

If friends didn't help each other in the time of crisis, who will?

Maybe tomorrow, someone else will help me when I land in a PIP.

Wishful thinking.

Hopeful, nevertheless.

CHAPTER TWENTY

THE ALPHA MALE

'Yes Ma'am, we can conclude the deal at Rs.14.5k, all inclusive of GST,' I said.

I was talking to Priya Amarnath, a Senior Software Engineer at a major tech multinational. She had an impressive background and profile, graduating from one of the top engineering institutes in India.

More than anything, she was a thorough professional throughout the deal. I enjoyed dealing with tough yet fair customers, who sought to derive value from a course rather than seeing it as just another monetary deal.

'Ok, thanks Surya. Appreciate your help. Can you send me the payment link?'

'Sure. I have to inform you that the payment link has a validity of only 15 minutes for security reasons. I would request you to complete the payment at the earliest.'

'I understand. Please share the link. I will be using my credit card to do the payment,' Priya said.

I generated the payment link, and shared the same over WhatsApp.

Priya acknowledged it with a yellow thumbs up. A notification popped up that she had landed on the payment gateway's homepage.

'So far, so good,' I whispered. She was now on the payment landing page, offering a variety of payment options.

I took a short break to get away from my laptop. 'No point staring at the screen, she would complete the payment.'

15 minutes passed. I had a glass of orange juice in my hand. Placing it on my study table, I hit the spacebar on my laptop to boot it up and check the status of the payment.

Shocking.

Priya had not gone beyond the card details page. Maybe there was a gateway or a bank issue? Or worse, she has decided to abandon her purchase midway.

This was common among many pots. They are all fired up about the course until they reach the Moment of Truth: completing the payment and watching the money leave their bank account.

But customers like Priya were different. I was ready to bet my incentive that she was going to take the course. The signals a customer provides in the first call gives a fair idea on what kind of person they are, as well as whether they are serious, or here for just timepass.

Instead of wasting time on rumination, I decided to call up Priya and find out myself.

'Hey Ma'am, Surya here. Any issues in the payment?'

There was a silence on the other line.

'Hello, Ma'am – are you there?'

A gruff voice answered my question.

'Hi, Sanjay here.'

'I'm sorry, who?' I blurted out.

'Sanjay Amarnath. Priya's husband, speaking.'

'I see. Hi Sir, how are you?'

He ignored my greeting. 'Resend the payment link to Priya. Make the course fee as 10k flat.'

My hand swung across the table in surprise, almost toppling my orange juice.

'Excuse me?' I asked.

'I said, re-send the course link to Priya with the revised fees of 10k.'

I could hear Priya on the other side of the line. 'God, Sanjay – can you stop this? Surya and I have already discussed everything. Why are you interfering...'

'Keep quiet. You don't know these sales agents, all wolves in sheep clothing. Can you sit tight while I do the negotiation?' Sanjay growled.

'Sir, with all due respect – Priya Ma'am negotiated quite well. I was really impressed by how...'

'Shut up. Did I ask you for a character certificate of my wife? Do as I tell you, or else consider this sale gone.'

Now that, pissed me off.

'I understand Sir. But I don't have the authority to change the payment amount. Why don't you talk to my manager?'

'I am ready to talk to anyone. Give him the phone.'

'Sure Sir. Give me two minutes time.'

I cut the call. So, this guy was a pseudo-Alpha male. Time, I made him understand he was nothing but a trial version of a Beta. I dialled Sanjay once again, from a different number.

'Hi Sanjay, Kapil here. Manager at Aspire. What's the problem?'

'Hello...Kapil. Hi, Sanjay here,' Sanjay did not expect the conversation to start in such a direct manner.

'Yes, I know that. I had to jump out of a meeting as Surya said it was urgent. What's the issue?'

'I want the course fee reduced.' Sanjay said.

'Are you the customer?'

'No, my wife is.'

'Then why are you talking on her behalf?'

A bead of sweat started to form on Sanjay's forehead. This conversation was not going the way he had envisioned.

'Well, I think...I believe...I mean, I have come to understand that the course fee for which the link was sent out, i.e. 14.5k, can be reduced further...'

'One second, Sanjay. Was the payment link shared with your wife?'

'Uhh...yes, it was.'

'Which means that, Surya has taken your wife's consent to share the link? This is standard operating procedure.'

'Yes, my wife confirmed verbally on call that the link could be shared.'

'Then boss, again I am asking you, what is your problem?' Kapil asked in an irritated tone.

'My problem?' Sanjay blinked.

'If your wife is ok to go ahead with the course, and has confirmed on call that the payment link can be shared, what is the issue here?'

'I believe I can negotiate a better deal...'

'There is no question of negotiating, Sanjay. A deal is a deal. We cannot re-share the payment link; it can be generated only once.'

'If you are not interested in the deal, I am fine with that. Have a good day. I am sorry to have wasted your time,' Kapil cut the call.

Sanjay could not believe what was happening. He was supposed to drive the conversation and bully me into getting more discount.

I dialled back Priya's number. This time, it was my normal voice.

'Hello Sir. Did you have a chance to talk to my manager?' I asked.

'Hi Surya, Priya here. I am so sorry for the confusion, this is embarrassing. Could you please talk to your tech team and send me an updated link for the price we discussed?'

'Oh ok, sure Ma'am. Let me check with the team once. What about Sir...?'

'Sir is now in the kitchen making orange juice for me. He will stay there until I say so,' she sounded very happy.

'Wow, what a coincidence, even I am drinking orange juice!'

'Ha ha, great. Please check and let me know, I will be waiting for an update from your end,' Priya ended the call.

Of course, we could generate another link. I wasted another twenty minutes before sharing the new payment link with Priya.

Within 30 seconds, the payment came through.

I rarely used the Kapil tactic. It was done when I came across an unreasonable and difficult customer. I drank another glass of orange juice. My throat was parched, talking like the aggressive Kapil as compared to my sweet and docile nature.

I hope Sanjay's juice was up to Priya's standard. Or else, he would be done for.

CHAPTER TWENTY-ONE

THE CROSS-SELL

It was Month End season.

'Stressful times, desperate measures,' is the motto on the lips of every salesperson in the company on Month Ends.

'Hi Karan, thanks for your time on the call. As discussed, you can avail the Scrum Master Certification at a final price of Rs.23,000 only, inclusive of GST.'

I was in talks with a customer, trying to close a deal to get me closer to my target.

'Ok, thanks Surya. Appreciate the detailed explanation about the course from your end. Any more discount possible? It's month end, after all,' Karan, an IT professional with over 15 years of experience, said.

'I understand, Karan. That is the expectation from all customers on Month Ends. Since we are not directly offering the course, rather – we are sourcing the course from a third-party vendor, we do not have a veto on the discounts. We have to sell at a pre-defined price only.'

'I see. Ok, no problem. Send me the link for payment.'

'Sure, can you...'

'Wait, one second. No, ignore what I just said. Send me the payment link at 8 PM tonight.'

I squirmed in my seat. It was now 10 AM in the morning. Typically, customers who say they will pay beyond a lead time of 3 hours, never do.

I tried to push him. 'Karan, this is a good offer. Why don't we make it official right away? Any questions you would like to ask me?'

'No, nothing Surya. I am satisfied with your approach and answers. Allow me some time, I will get back to you today.'

One last try. 'Karan, is it a bank or credit card issue? We have other payment options as well for your consideration.'

'Surya, I told you right? I will get back to you. Wait for my ping or call, bye,' Karan cut the call abruptly.

Well, it was my duty to try.

I looked up his mail id. '*karanbiswas129@gmail.com.*'

'Phone number: 9994442200.'

'Alright, let him call me. Until then, let me look at any over dues and hunt on them,' I said to myself.

Month Ends are very different from other days. On a normal day, time would go at a snail's pace and you would pray for the day to come to an end as quickly as possible. Any month end has never been less than an adventure for me, there has always been one story or the other to tell. Time flies at an eagle's pace and as a salesperson, you are only playing catchup with the clock and your target.

'Surya, it's already 5 PM. When is that Scrum Master payment going to come through?' Vijay asked.

Shit, I had completely forgot about Karan. He was supposed to ping me when he was ready to do the payment. As is always, the sales team had to inform Vijay on any potential payments coming their way as and when we were sure we could close the pot.

I had confidently stated that Karan was a sure-shot payment, and boasted to Vijay that I would close him by evening. It was a different matter altogether that I had forgotten all about it.

'Yes, Vijay. I am working on it. The customer had insisted that I share him the payment link by 8 PM tonight. Don't worry, it will be done.'

Vijay was on video. He rarely switched on his camera.

I could see his left eye twitch. Ok, that was not a good sign.

It was Vijay's sixth sense tingling.

'Listen, Surya. What did you say the customer's name was?'

'Karan. Karan Biswas. He's an IT professional looking for the Scrum Master course, weekend batch. Nice chap.'

Vijay did not say anything for a full two minutes. He seemed to be clicking away at his laptop furiously. I sensed that something was wrong.

'Vijay, can I get back to calling? I have a few pots to close by the end of the hour, so...'

Suddenly, Vijay looked at me directly. His face was a mix of fury and disgust.

'Those bastards...I am cutting the call. Bye, talk to you later,' Vijay cut the call abruptly.

I was perplexed. 'What transpired in the last two minutes for Vijay to go offline? It was not in his character,' I mused.

I saw a notification pop up. It was Vijay.

'A cross-sell has happened on your pot - Karan. He has already purchased the course from another agent.'

A cross-sell is when a sales agent poaches a client from another agent through unethical means, usually by enticing the client with more discounts or complementary products. A colloquial word for 'cross-sell' would be 'cutting.'

I could not believe what was happening. I called Vijay immediately.

'Vijay, what are you saying? That's not possible. The guy has only one set of credentials and, I have it with me right now...'

'Cut your crying. Figure out what to do now. Search for this mail id in the CRM right away: _itguy_biswaskaran@gmail.com_.'

My fingers flew across the keyboard. I saw the details flash on the screen.

'Hey one second, this pot is showing as 'Closed Won.' The sale was made by Rajat.' I re-checked the details. The sale was made exactly 10 minutes after my call with Karan today morning. There was a different number associated with the email id as well.

'Vijay, what do I do?' I groaned. I felt I was getting stupider at this job; anyone could fool me.

'Did I not tell you to stop crying? Listen to me carefully.'

'You were the first person he was in contact with, right? Check the lead creation time.'

I opened the CRM page. The email id assigned to me – '_karanbiswas129@gmail.com_' was assigned to me on the 25th of the month at 5.30 PM.

'The lead assigned to me was created on the 25th,' I said.

'Fine. Now check, when the lead was created in the system for the mail id – '_itguy_biswaskaran@gmail.com_.'

I ran a quick query. The result was alarming.

The lead was created at 10:10 AM, today morning.

'Vijay, how are you sure this is a cross-sell? They could be two different guys as well.'

'I am going on a hunch. This is the same guy. Do one thing, call Karan right now and put him on speaker. Let's hear what he has to say.'

I woke up my phone and punched in Karan's name in my contact list. He picked up after three rings.

'Hi Karan, how are you doing today?'

'I'm doing good, Surya. Thanks for asking. How are you?'

'Doing good, thanks. Karan, I am calling with regards to the Scrum Master course – we had discussed that we would close the deal at 8 PM today. Apologies for advancing our call. If you are free, could we proceed with the enrolment?'

There was silence on the other end.

So, Vijay was bang on.

'Yeah...regarding that, I was about to call you, Surya. I have decided to postpone the Scrum Master certification by six months. I have just been pulled into a new project by my company and it would not be feasible for me to start something new altogether.'

'That's not surprising,' I murmured.

'I'm sorry?'

'No, what I meant was – you can purchase the course at the discussed price right now. Later on, you may start the course at a date of your convenience.'

It was a phone call, yet I was pretty sure he was sweating profusely at the other end of the line.

'Umm...not really, Surya. Maybe some other time. I will get back to you on this. Good day to you,' Karan was about to hang up the call.

That was when, I drew my master weapon.

'Rajat is being asked to reverse the Scrum Master course payment as of this very moment. The payment will come to me now, since I was the first point of contact for your lead. But this is a cross-sell, which is not tolerated in this company.'

'Rajat's services as an Inside Sales Manager are being terminated with immediate effect. I had called to inform you regarding the same.'

'Have a good day, Karan. Wishing you well.'

I could hear a startled yelp on the other line.

'Surya, wait! One second, just one second,' Karan said.

'Sure Karan, tell me. How can I help you?'

'Surya, listen. I'm sorry, I gave an alternate mail id and negotiated with Rajat to get a better deal on the Scrum Master course. I wanted to be a different identity to you, that's all...Rajat promised me that I would get a free course as well if I went with him by cutting you...I did not know that this would result in a termination of any sort...'

'I understand, Karan. But policy is policy.'

'Yes, yes...absolutely, as it should be. I'm sorry, did you mention that my payment is now under you?'

'Yes, I did.'

'Which means, you can help me with the free course?'

I grabbed my headphone's mike and closed it with my fist. I fell off my chair laughing out loud. How the hunter, had become the hunted.

'My apologies, Karan; I don't seem to follow. What free course?'

'Rajat told me that I would get a free Python Scripting course with my purchase.'

'That's a question you have to ask Rajat, not me.'

'But, but...you have got my payment.'

'Absolutely, as per company policy. Since Rajat initiated a cross-sell. Therefore, the payment goes to the agent who contacted the customer first.'

Karan's voice started to shake with anger. 'I don't care about your company's internal policies. I was promised a free course, and I want it at any cost.'

'And, what do you have to say about Rajat's termination?'

'That's a risk he was well aware of before going ahead with the deal. I am sorry to hear about this, my sympathies are with him,' Karan said in a flat tone.

Here was a customer with no conscience.

'Right. Do you have any proof of this 'free-course' you are talking about?'

'I remember Rajat speaking to me about it on call...'

'I see. He must have called you from Aspire's official number? I can extract the recording, then.'

There was a contained silence at the other end.

'No, it was a WhatsApp call from his personal number.'

I pounced on his point. 'Which means to say, you have no proof whatsoever that a deal was promised to you either on mail, WhatsApp or text?'

'I don't care. He must stand by his word.'

'Why don't you add him to this call? We can clear things up.'

'Yes, wait...I have his number...I am adding him now.'

Rajat joined the call immediately. We were on a conference call now.

'Hi Rajat, Karan here.'

Rajat wasn't too happy to see me in the call.

'Hi Karan, what is Surya doing here in this call? I thought it was only you who was calling me.'

'I asked Surya to join this call to clear the confusion regarding the Scrum Master course. Rajat, you had sent me the payment link for Rs. 21,000 today morning, right?'

Rajat squirmed. He knew he had screwed up big time, and the big bosses wouldn't be happy. A cross-sell, along with underselling a third-party course? Best recipe for disaster.

'Umm...Karan, can we take this offline?'

Karan was adamant. 'No, Rajat. Let's clear things up. You had sent me the link today morning, right?'

'Yes, I did.'

'Ok fine. Surya is now telling me that he has my payment, but will not give me the free course you said will be provided to me, if I enrolled with you.'

Rajat's eyebrows shot up. 'Karan, what free course are you talking about?'

'Python Scripting. We spoke about this on call, don't you remember?'

Rajat knew he was in the wrong. He went into complete denial mode.

'Karan, I'm sorry but I think you are confusing my call with a one you had with some other agent. We cannot provide free courses with the Scrum Master.'

Karan started to protest. 'Hey, just a second buddy...wait...'

'Karan, I have another call to attend to. Surya will help you with all your queries hereon.'

'Have a good day.'

'RAJAT! WHERE THE HELL DO YOU THINK YOU ARE GOING? I want my free course, or else I will take all of you to the consumer court,' Karan bellowed.

Rajat spoke in a calm voice. 'Go ahead. There is no proof I have promised anything. I did say I will enable a complimentary course on a WhatsApp call, so which means there is no evidence I've said anything.'

'And what about your termination?'

Now was Rajat's turn to become shocked.

'What termination?

'Surya told me you are being terminated for doing a cross-sell.'

'Utter bullshit, did he say that? I am doing double my target this month, why will I get fired? Surya, what are you...'

I ended the call. The entire call recording would be delivered to my inbox in about 10 minutes time. Rajat would be lucky if he would hang on to his job post today's meeting.

I had called Karan's bluff regarding the termination. Nether Karan or Rajat knew that the phone call was being recorded.

Not the most ethical way of doing things, but hey – to survive in sales, one can't be a straight shooter.

'Good job on the recording, Surya. Rajat has been given a stern warning,' Vijay said.

I was baffled. 'Stern warning? That's it?'

'Yeah. He has done double his target this month, so has been awarded the 'Star Performer' this time round.'

'Seriously? And what about me?'

'You? You didn't do your target, neither did you sell the Scrum Master course at the designated price.'

'Vijay, I didn't sell it. Rajat did.'

'Doesn't matter. The payment is now under your name. You want to be a crusader for the truth, be my guest. Get your target done first before you want to flaunt your moral values to other sales agents.'

'Thanks Vijay. You made my day,' I said drily.

'Hey, don't blame me. I just run the numbers. Get me the sales, I'm happy. You don't? I will make you unhappy.'

'Bye Vijay, I really don't know how you can live with yourself.'

'I just bought an iPhone last month, and a bike the month before that. I think I live with myself pretty well.'

I had no response.

CHAPTER TWENTY-TWO

FARZII

'Surya, I want the course at 12k flat, give it to me right now.'

I was handling a difficult customer. Noel thought that Aspire was his Dad's company.

'Noel, try to understand. I cannot provide the course at such a low price. It is against our company policy. More ever, why don't you look at the value we are providing? The CTC you will get after doing this course will more than compensate what you are currently going to purchase at Aspire.'

'Don't give me *gyaan*, Surya. Do your job. Send me the link for 12k.'

'Noel, I can't do that; I have already told you.'

'I want to talk to your manager,' Noel gritted his teeth.

I was not in a mood to change my voice; my throat was completely out. Anyway, this guy did not seem like he was going to budge from his stance.

'The Manager is not available. He is honeymooning with his wife in the Maldives.'

'I don't care if he is climbing the Himalayas with one finger. Call him, and get him on the line for me. Don't you guys respect customers?'

Yeah, we do. Just not you.

I closed my eyes. 'Let me try, one last time.'

'Noel, for the last time. We cannot sell the course at 12k. You are asking for too much discount, which is not permitted. I will lose my job if I have to sell it to you at this price.'

'Why do I care? You salespeople will find another job anyway. Send me the link right now.'

That's when, I blew my top.

'You *chindi* loser...who do you think you are? I am telling you, again and again; there is no discount available, do you not understand?' I shouted.

Noel was taken aback.

'One second...did you just call me *chindi*?'

I had said loser also. Did he miss that part?

'Yes, I did. You are haggling with me like this is a vegetable market.'

'I...I...do you know who I am?' Noel said indignantly.

'I know who you are. You're a cheap, pathetic person who doesn't treat the person you are speaking to as a human being.'

'The bigger question is – Do YOU know who you are?'

Noel rebutted with such ferocity; I was taken aback.

'How dare you call me cheap! How dare...I drive a Mercedes, top of the range! You wait, just you wait...' Noel abruptly cut the call.

Well, another complaint in my cap. Just another day at work.

I was looking at another pot's details, when Prem pinged me.

'Broo...did you see? Did you see?'

'Hey Prem. What are you talking about?' I pinged back.

'Surya, check your pot's status. The Noel guy; Python Programming.'

I checked Noel's status in the CRM. It showed 'Closed Won.' It showed me as the owner of the pot.

'What the...Prem, I never sent this guy a link.'

'Did you connect with him?'

Yes, I did. We had an, uhh...altercation.'

'The guy has paid full price on the website. Full 23k bro. Rich guy, it seems,' Prem yelped.

He did say he had a Mercedes.

'So, it's a Farzii,' I said.

'No, it's not, it's a semi-Farzii,' Prem pinged.

'How da?'

'If you did not connect with the pot beforehand, then it's a Farzii. You spoke to him, so it's a semi-Farzii.'

'Fine, whatever. Payment is a payment.'

I heard my phone ping. Noel had pinged me on WhatsApp.

'Surya, look at this screenshot. I have paid full price for the course. *Chindi*, am I?'

I stifled my laughter. I pinged back.

'Hi Noel, that's great. Hope you enjoy the course. Can you send me a picture of your Mercedes as well?'

'You want to see that? You think I'm bluffing?' Noel pinged back.

'I just want to see the colour of the car,' I messaged.

'You doubt me? Wait, I will show you now.'

Noel sent me a few pictures. Yes, he did own a Mercedes.

Well, let me try one more thing.

'Noel, would you say you are rich?'

'Yes, I am very rich. I have a house right next to the Governor's house.'

'Is it? Well...I don't think you are as wealthy as to buy our Masters in Python course. Do you think you can afford it?'

Noel flared up again. 'You doubt me, again? You just wait, I will buy that course as well and shove the receipt in your face.'

The next day, Vijay was left wondering on how I was able to generate revenue worth over 1 lakh in a single day.

I smiled. Who says angry people are unproductive?

CHAPTER TWENTY-THREE

LEAVING

People think that landing a job is tough.

I disagree. That's the easy part.

Every tried leaving?

'Abhishek Sir, I want to do my MBA. Can you please relieve me? I have dropped my papers already,' I wailed on call.

'Nothing doing. Who the heck is going to do your target for the rest of the month? Will I sit, and do it?' Abhishek screamed.

Maybe you should, I thought to myself.

'Did you say I should do your target?' Abhishek glared.

'No, no Sir...I didn't say anything,'

'And what will come any good of doing an MBA? I don't have an MBA, and I'm a Manager at Aspire. See? It's the skills that matter in life, not the degree.'

'*Chamchagiri* is not a skill, Abhishek,' I muttered to myself.

'What was that?' Abhishek screamed.

'Sir, what face will I show to society?'

'Are you, my boss? Do I have to answer your questions?'

'Sorry Sir. I shouldn't have spoken like that to you,' I was nursing a bad headache. Now was not the time to negotiate or plead with Abhishek.

I summoned upon myself a year's worth of anger, frustration, guilt and sleepless nights to the fore. I was going to tell this man what I really thought of him, whether he accepted my resignation or not.

'You listen to me, you...' I was interrupted by a loud ping.

It was my Gmail inbox.

I couldn't believe it. I read the subject line.

'Resignation accepted. Wishing you all the very best. Regards, Abhishek.'

I fumbled for words. 'Abhishek Sir, how...why? I mean...'

Abhishek smiled, a rare smile for a guy who terrorized me for a year.

'How many salespeople do you think I've seen at my time in Aspire? Hundreds. How many have I seen leaving? About the same number.'

'I know I may have not been the best super boss you might have wanted. But I understand the need to pursue one's goals in life.'

'Yes, I have accepted your resignation. Serve your notice period, then you can leave.'

My ears turned red, and a sense of shame overcame me. 'Was I just about to abuse this guy? What a sweetheart.'

'By the way, have you decided on what you are going to specialize, in your MBA?'

'Finance, Sir.'

'Is it? I thought you were more of a marketing guy. Not a very aggressive one, more of the softer types.'

'Soft, Sir?'

'Yeah, you know – not overly trying to push the customer to buy a course, or attempt any means possible to get a sale done. I was after your life so that it would make you a sharper salesman. Don't take it personally.'

I stayed quiet. Let the compliments flow while they could.

'Your biggest strength is your ability to make the customer trust you. I hope you maintain this with your future bosses as well.'

'All the very best, Surya. Godspeed.'

He was in a very good mood. Now was a good time to drop the bombshell.

'Abhishek Sir?'

'Hm? Anything else? I thought our business was done, right?' Abhishek said, without looking up from a plate of papaya he was eating.

'Yes, almost done. I can't serve the notice period.'

Abhishek spat out the papaya, his spit spraying all over his laptop screen. His eyes bulged wide and stared into my soul.

'Why the hell not?' he screamed.

'My college starts in 5 days. I had put it in my resignation mail, did you not notice?'

I had deliberately put the start date of my college in small letters and hidden it amongst a bunch of resignation jargon and thank you notes. In between the lines, I had requested Abhishek to relieve me of the mandatory notice period.

Now, I had an official mail from my super boss, stating that my resignation was approved.

'You, you scumbag, I will...'

'Abhishek, you can't do anything. HR is also copied on this mail. *Chalo*, see you then.'

His eyes widened. No sales agent had ever called him by his first name.

'Don't you dare cut the call! I will make a mincemeat out of you,' Abhishek bellowed.

'it's Covid, Abhishek. Remember? We are still under the nationwide lockdown.' I smirked.

'I am reversing my acceptance. No way you are leaving Aspire under my watch.'

'Too late. I have your proof of acceptance on email. Before I go, I have to say something...'

'Yeah? What's that?'

I closed my eyes, and recalled Ajith's favourite dialogue.

'Bye, now.'

About The Author

Shiva Shankar Iyer is an alumnus of the Masters of Business Administration Program at CHRIST University. He has completed his Bachelors in Industrial and Production Engineering from The National Institute of Engineering, Mysuru. He has cleared the prestigious UGC-NET Examination in the first attempt and has secured a score among the Top 2.5% in the country.

He has previously worked with an Education Tech company in the capacity of an Inside Sales Manager, and is currently pursuing a career in Finance.

Shiva has previously authored two books – '#GoodForNothingNalayak (2018)' and 'The Nalayak Returns (2021)', both of which focus on the problems and dilemma faced by the Indian youth.

Apart from writing, Shiva is passionate about exploring new places, world economics and learning martial arts.